# HIJACKED

# HIJACKED
By David Harper

DODD, MEAD & COMPANY

New York

ISBN 0-396-06197-4
Library of Congress Catalog Card Number: 78-123502
Printed in the United States of America
by Vail-Ballou Press, Inc., Binghamton, N. Y.

TO ROD AND NOEL

# HIJACKED

## PROLOGUE

The Boeing 707 jet had been fueled and cleaned after its last flight.

At six-thirty in the morning, it was towed to the loading ramp at Gate Five of Trans-America's main concourse at John F. Kennedy International Airport on Long Island.

This ship, tail number N38100D, was Trans-America's Flight 901, nonstop from New York to San Francisco. The early morning sun glinted on silver wings that spanned 130 feet from tip to tip.

Takeoff was scheduled for 7:55 A.M.

Flight 901 would leave late. And it would never reach San Francisco.

An hour before takeoff, surrounded by hundreds of people who saw—and yet, saw nothing—the hijacker stopped at the concourse's drugstore and purchased a tube of orange-colored Revlon lipstick, then went into the snack bar and sipped coffee nervously, waiting.

1

## THE FIRST HOUR

"Ninety-six booked," said the Flight Dispatcher. "That's not good. Pass the word. No standbys this morning. Even if only ninety show, we're in trouble."

"What's our FOD at San Francisco?" asked Sam Allen, First Officer of Trans-America Flight 901.

"Fuel over destination, 32,000 pounds," said the Dispatcher. "Weather there's lousy. If it closes in, you'll have to divert to Reno."

"Why not Portland?"

"Weather Control says if the front socks San Francisco in, Portland'll go too."

The young First Officer sighed deliberately. "Captain O'Hara's going to be mighty unhappy about this," he said. "He hasn't diverted a flight since he started flying jets."

The Dispatcher shrugged. "What do you want from me?" he asked good-naturedly. "I only report the condi-

3

tions, I don't make them. Your empty weight is just under 120,000 pounds; payload of 22,000; 32,000 pounds of fuel over destination. Another 71,000 for the flight—you'll be bucking a loop of the jet stream over Kansas, remember. That adds up to 245,000 pounds gross. If I wanted to be mean I'd reduce that to 240,000 and take off the mail."

"You're all heart," said Sam Allen, picking up his battered flight bag. "Well, the Oracle has spoken. The explosion you hear from the Crew's Lounge in three minutes will be Michael O'Hara kicking his poor First Officer through the overhead."

"Why the big fuss? O'Hara got a girl friend in San Francisco?"

"In Portland," Allen replied. "His daughter."

Angela Shaw looked at the slim Lady Hamilton watch encircling her tanned wrist. Ten after seven in the morning and she had been up since four. The blond stewardess stifled a yawn. Going all the way out to Montauk the night before a flight had been foolish. But Paul Manchester was scheduled for a trip to Caracas to take a hard look at his advertising agency's branch office there and would be gone before Angie got back from her turnaround in San Francisco.

"Paul," she had complained, "why Montauk? It takes forever to drive and I've got to be on deck at Kennedy at 6:00 A.M."

"I've got my reasons," he said, grinning like a little boy instead of a six-foot, forty-one-year-old vice president of a Madison Avenue advertising agency.

"I won't even be able to have a martini with you," she went on. "You know I can't drink twenty-four hours before a flight."

"A light rosé wine," he said softly. "Clorets for the breath. No one will ever know."

"They turn your tongue green," she said, smiling in spite of herself. "Miss Martin checks if she's suspicious."

Paul was incredulous. "You mean she has you stick out your tongue?"

"Sordid, isn't it? Wait until I'm a Head Stewardess. I'll—"

The game was out of hand. Helplessly, they broke into laughter.

Later, curled up on a big rug before the fireplace in the Montauk cabin, he handed her the tiny jewelry box without a word. Dinner had been steaks broiled on the beach, served with a crisp salad and a nicely chilled bottle of rosé. Now, in front of the fire, he sipped on a martini as Angie nursed a final glass of wine.

"Paul—" she began, without opening the box.

"Don't say anything, Angie," he said. "Just open it."

"Don't spoil things," she pleaded. "We've talked about this before. You know how I feel—"

"Angie," he said, touching her empty hand, "time's rushing by. I want us to share it together."

"We *are* together . . ."

"Sure, like soldiers on a weekend pass," he said almost bitterly. "I share you with Miss Martin and that damned Boeing 707. You're regimented and supervised like a schoolgirl. Not allowed to drink, not allowed to let your hair grow long, not allowed marry and still keep your job—"

"Darling," she said, kissing his hand, "I don't want to quit flying yet. And you're right, if I get married, Trans-America will take me off flight status. It's an archaic rule, I know—and most of the other airlines have already abol-

5

ished it. Some of the girls marry secretly, but that's not for me. If I were Mrs. Paul Manchester, I'd want to shout my new name at the whole world."

"If you were," he said, "you'd be going to Caracas with me tomorrow instead of serving steaks and cleaning up after drunks all across America."

"Give me more time," she pleaded, holding the unopened box out to him. "There's a rumor the rule will be changed as part of our next contract with management. Or anything might happen."

Silently he took the velvet box, slipped it into his pocket. His voice, when it came, was expressionless:

"Do you want me to drive you back tonight?"

Angela shook her head slowly. "No, Paul. I want to stay with you."

Now, on duty for over an hour at only ten after seven, she hid another yawn. The standard joke among stewardesses was, "Boy, am I tired. I walked clean across the United States today."

Tired as Angela Shaw felt, it did not seem funny anymore.

"But I'll miss my shipment," the young soldier said desperately.

The slim, red-headed ticket clerk smiled sympathetically. "I'm sorry," she said. "But we've been notified not to accept standby passengers for Flight 901. You see, sir, your special military fare is on a space available basis—and I'm afraid there just isn't any available on this particular flight. Now if you don't mind taking our Flight 816 later today—"

"That'll be too late," he said. "I'm supposed to report at

0700 this morning."

The clerk looked at the big clock with its red sweep second hand. "It's already seven-fifteen," she said. "And the flight takes five hours . . ."

"But there's a three-hour time difference," the soldier said rapidly. "Sure, I'll report in an hour or so late, but I won't miss the shipment. The worst I'd get is company punishment. But for missing a move—" The young soldier spread his hands helplessly.

"I'm very sorry, sir," the girl said, "but there just isn't anything I—"

A bluff, heavy-set man standing behind the soldier leaned forward. "Miss," he said, "why don't you check this with your supervisor? There must be some way to help this young man."

"We're very busy, sir—" she began.

"Congressman," he corrected. "Congressman Arne Lindner of Wisconsin. Would you please call your supervisor?"

Flustered, the clerk said, "Yes, sir—I mean, Congressman. Excuse me." She hurried away.

"Thanks, sir," said the young soldier. "It's all my fault. I cut things too close. But I'm scheduled for overseas shipment, and I wanted that one last night at home."

"I know just how you feel, son," said the Congressman. "I put in a little AWOL time myself once a long time ago. My excuse wasn't even an extra night at home. I got mixed up in an all-night crap game and I was winning and didn't want to leave."

The young soldier laughed. "Was that Vietnam, sir?" he asked.

Surprised, the Congressman shook his head. "No," he

7

said gently, "it was in a war you wouldn't even remember. They called it World War Two."

The huge jet was empty when Flight Engineer John Bimonte undogged the forward hatch and went aboard. In his hand was a clipboard holding a printed Flight Engineer's Preflight Inspection sheet. In the next forty minutes, he would check off 214 separate items, ranging from radio and navigational equipment to the supply of fresh water for the flush toilets in the lounges.

Bimonte was so familiar with the list that he could have recited it backward from memory. But he still examined every item on the printed form carefully and checked it off methodically.

With more than two thousand hours as a Navy jet pilot, Bimonte had hoped to make the transition to civilian piloting after his discharge. But the years after the Korean conflict were crowded with ex-military pilots, and rather than go into general aviation Bimonte had joined Trans-America knowing that he could never progress beyond Flight Engineer. Secretly he was relieved. In the few occasions during his military career when he had been forced to exercise command decision, he had found the experience lonely and disturbing. A careful, punctual man, he was most at home executing orders given by others. As such, with his vast knowledge of flying, he made a superb Flight Engineer—a fact that had not been lost upon the company's personality testing staff when he first applied for employment.

His stubby fingers expertly flicked dozens of switches in the crowded flight deck as he recorded readings from the confusing array of instruments. As his stomach rumbled, he thought half-consciously of breakfast. On an early flight like 901, he never bothered to eat at home. The extra time was well spent in the king-sized bed with his plumpish wife, Martha. The ritual was always the same. As his hand stroked the soft mound below the concealing blanket, she whispered, "Johnny, I've got to fix breakfast." And he always answered, "Don't worry about it, honey. The stews take good care of me." Her answer was, "That's what I'm afraid of—the kind of care they'll take." "In that case," he would say, "maybe you'd better see if you can simmer down the old fire before I report in." And in the predawn grayness of Bensonhurst, the big bed began to move in the slow, steady rhythm of the sea . . .

Bimonte's mind snapped back to the check list. He could not remember whether he had examined the Number Two engine's water pressure. Silently he moved his lips in a curse. Got to watch that stuff, he thought. Go fooling around remembering this morning, and I'll miss something important and catch hell from O'Hara. He repeated the last three items on the check list, just to be sure.

Hazel Martin, Head Stewardess of Flight 901 by virtue of six years of seniority, tapped her foot as Jane Burke hurried into the Crew Lounge.

"Sorry I'm late, Hazel," said the younger girl. "The taxi broke down on the Triborough Bridge and—"

"You have to learn to allow for those unexpected things," Hazel said, trying to put the right mixture of stern admonition and fairness into her voice. It was no picnic, being in charge of three other stewardesses on a transcontinental flight. There was so much to be done, and so little time in which to do it . . .

9

"I'll be more careful," Jane Burke promised. "Are the other girls here?"

"*They* were on time," Hazel Martin said. "You'd better check with registrations. They've got two passengers flagged for kosher meals. Make sure the trays get on board."

Jane giggled. "I was just thinking—"

"What?" Hazel's voice was harsh.

"How do they know? I mean, who can tell a kosher steak from the ones we get from the regular caterer? it isn't like they stamp them with a big K or something."

Hazel's lips tightened. "Jane, your attitude leaves something to be desired," she said. "It's none of our concern what a passenger's religion—"

"All right, all right! Don't make a federal case out of it. I'm on my way."

The young stewardess hurried away. Hazel Martin looked after her and shook her head.

It was hard to believe that she herself had ever been so young.

"Don't hang up!" Elly Brewster screamed at the operator. "I don't have another dime!"

"I am sorry," said the impersonal voice, "but your party does not wish to accept the charges."

"Can't you try again? I'm at the airport and I'm broke and—"

There was a pause, then, "Very well. I will try once more. Just a minute, please."

Elly heard faint beeping sounds, a buzzing noise, then a click. "714th Replacement Depot, Sergeant Lipscomb speaking," said a deep male voice.

"I have a collect call for Airman First Class Charles

Reynolds," said the operator.

Elly cut in, "Sergeant, please tell him it's important. I'm trying to get out there, but I don't have any money and—"

"Sorry, ma'am," said the male voice. "Airman Reynolds has instructed me to refuse any calls from New York. Goodbye."

The line went dead. "I am sorry," said the operator, "but your party—"

"Oh, go to hell!" said Elly Brewster and hung up.

"Here's the dispatcher's flight plan," Sam Allen said, handing a sheaf of papers to Michael O'Hara.

The Captain, a slim, gray-haired man in his middle fifties nodded. "They're worried about weather," he said.

"How did you know?"

"You can smell it around the place. They're costing out the flight and seeing red ink everywhere. I swear to God, every time they take a pallet of cargo off, the front office goes into shock."

His First Officer grinned. "Here's the teletype from Upper Air Center."

O'Hara took the yellow strip of paper. It read:

FLT AVG TAS 485 KTS AND 245 TAKEOFF WT. OPTM
OFF-ON 4+51 ALT 32T VIA JR 78 CLE JR 82

Translated, the message meant that, basing the figures on an average flight speed of 485 knots, with a takeoff weight of 245,000 pounds, the estimated time from takeoff to landing would be four hours, fifty-one minutes. The altitude assigned was 32,000 feet and the flight path suggested was jet route 78 to Cleveland, where he would

11

pick up jet route 82 on into San Francisco.

O'Hara scowled and looked at the next line:

JFK TOC -16 245/40 -35

"Top of climb temperature is minus sixteen Centigrade," he told his First Officer. "And there's a wind out of 245 degrees averaging forty knots. That's going to cut down our true air speed by thirty-five knots."

"We're going out light," said Allen. "And they're not taking any standbys."

"Go get some coffee, Sam," said O'Hara. "I want to check these figures over again. With a front moving in on the Coast, I don't know if we're going out at all."

Sam Allen stared at his Captain. "You mean you'd cancel?" he asked.

"Why not? Would you rather divert to Reno, Nevada?"

Sam shrugged, and headed for the coffee line.

The man who had introduced himself as Congressman Arne Lindner excused himself and went to one of the coin lockers beside the entrance to the men's room. He inserted a key, unlocked one of the lockers, and took out a long canvas-and-leather case. He hefted it, looked around, then deliberately wrapped his raincoat around it and, making the object as inconspicuous as possible, returned to the loading gate.

"Now, don't you worry," Harriet Stevens told her mother as a clerk attached a San Francisco baggage tag to her suitcase and placed in on a moving belt behind the check-in counter. "I'll be able to catch a shuttle flight up to Seattle. I'd rather do that than wait around here an-

12

other seven hours."

The older woman looked at Harriet's bulging maternity dress. "I don't know, dear," she said. "What did he say in that telephone call to make you decide to leave in such a hurry? And if you don't mind my saying so, you've been acting strangely." The young woman raised her hand, and her mother hurried to say, "What if something goes wrong while you're up in the air? I wish you'd change your mind."

"Mama, my suitcase is already gone. And besides, I want to be with Harry when the baby comes. If I'd known this trip East was going to keep me here so long I wouldn't have come at all."

"But your father's illness—"

"Mama, I came, didn't I? And Daddy's all right now, so I'm going home. Just please, don't worry! I'll be in Seattle tonight if I have to hijack the plane."

"Don't joke about things like that," said her mother.


"No more for me," groaned William Reading. It was almost three in the morning in Fairbanks, Alaska, and the young FBI man planned to go bear hunting at dawn on this, the first day of the season.

"One more," said his host, Assistant Police Chief Hugh Thomas, popping the tops of two more cans of Rainier Beer. "You're ten bucks ahead and I want to get it back."

"What fun is two-handed poker?" complained Reading. "I should have left with the rest of the guys."

"Listen," said Thomas, "how often is it that *both* our wives are down in Seattle for a week? Let's take advantage and hoot and holler a little."

"You hoot and holler all you want to," said the FBI man. "As for me, I am going to hit the rack. I've spent all week sighting in that damned rifle and I intend to get me a big brown bear come first light. Thanks for the poker game, buddy, and I'll see you when I get back."

"Chicken," growled Hugh Thomas. Reading sank down in the canvas-backed folding chair. Something prodded him and he reached back to remove it.

"How about that," he mumbled, looking down at the Police Special, surprised. "Clean forgot I was wearing it."

It was now 7:40 A.M. at John F. Kennedy International Airport, and the loudspeakers announced, "Trans-America Flight 901 is now boarding at Gate Five in the Main Concourse. All aboard, please."

Specialist Five Jerry Weber waited at the gate, anxiously shifting from one foot to another.

"We'll do our best, sir," the gate surpervisor had told Congressman Arne Lindner. "If there are any cancellations whatsoever, the young man will get the first seat."

"I'll get a general court if I miss that movement," Weber said in an undertone.

"What about baggage?" asked the gate supervisor.

"Just this little one," said the young soldier. "I'll carry it."

"Well," said the supervisor, hesitating. "Good luck."

"Don't worry, son," said the Congressman. "There are always a couple of No-Shows."

"I hope so." said Weber.

"Good morning, sir," said Hazel Martin, smiling at the first passenger to enter the airplane. She looked at his boarding pass and said, "That's through the first compartment and halfway to the rear."

Beside her, Angela Shaw smiled too and said nothing.

14

Jane Burke and the trainee, Lovejoy Welles, were in the rear, Tourist Class compartment. Lovejoy had announced her name to Jane with an almost defiant, I-dare-you-to-laugh stare. Jane bit the inside of her lip and kept a straight face. "Well," she whispered later to Angela, "it's better than Ladybird."

As the ship filled, the flight crew came aboard. O'Hara nodded brusquely at the stewardesses and entered the flight deck without a word. John Bimonte followed, intent on his final check list. Sam Allen paused near Angela and murmured, "We just about didn't make it, baby."

Surprised, she asked, "Make what?"

"O'Hara almost canceled us out. He doesn't like the weather on the Coast, and our alternate is Reno, Nevada."

She laughed. "I don't blame him," she said. "I'd cancel out too if it was a choice between canceling and Reno."

"Shhh!" hissed Hazel Martin. Another passenger entered and she beamed at him. "Good morning, sir," she said. "First Class? Miss Shaw will show you to your seat."

"This way, sir," said Angie. The man followed her, looking around nervously.

Sam Allen grinned and went forward to the flight deck.

Flight 901 was scheduled to leave at 7:55 A.M. That time was less than five minutes away, and every reservation except for one party of two had been claimed and the passengers were aboard the aircraft.

"They're pretty late," the Congressman said hopefully. "I bet they don't show."

"They'll show," said the young soldier bitterly. "The way my luck's been running, they'll show at exactly one minute before I get aboard."

The Congressman started to say something to cheer up the boy, but before he was able to utter a word there was a commotion in the crowded concourse and a tremendously large black man mashed his way through the aisle like a linebacker rushing the passer. He carried an hourglass-shaped leather case almost as large as himself.

"Just made it!" he announced to the surprised gate supervisor. "The name's Brown—Boo Brown."

The supervisor looked at his list. "Yes, sir," he said, "we have you listed. Is there anyone with you?"

"Traveling Single-O, daddy."

"In that case, shall we cancel the other reservation you are holding?"

Eagerly Specialist Five Jerry Weber stepped forward.

"Does that mean there's room for me?" he asked.

"Hold on, man," said Boo Brown to the supervisor, "I may be traveling alone, but I need that other seat."

Appraising the man's girth, the supervisor smiled and said, "Yes, sir, I can see what you mean. But the First Class seats are quite large enough—"

"Not for me, man. For my horn!"

"Your what?"

The black man's hamlike hand slapped the cello case.

"My horn, daddy. Like, my cello. I bought me an extra seat to strap Mama in alongside old Boo."

"I've heard you play," began the Congressman, "and first let me say it's a rare honor to meet you. Now, it seems this young man has a problem—"

"Mister Brown," said Jerry Weber, "I've got to get on that plane. I mean, if I don't, they'll keep me in the stockade until I grow a long white beard. I've already been in trouble twice. The next time they'll throw the book at me."

16

The black musician looked from the soldier to the Congressman to the gate supervisor and said, "Will somebody explain this gig to me?"

Quietly Congressman Arne Lindner described Weber's plight. When he finished, Boo Brown gave a wide grin and bellowed, "Well, sure, man! Can't let the troops down. We'll stash Mama in one of the johns and—"

"I'll have your instrument placed in the baggage compartment, Mr. Brown," the gate supervisor said, reaching for it.

Boo Brown drew back. "No you don't, buster," he said. "Mama don't travel in no baggage compartment. This here horn was put together in Italy in the eighteenth century and you couldn't pay for her with ten years' salary. As far as I know, she's the only one still outside a museum. She goes with me."

"I'm afraid there isn't any place in the cabin to store your—ah—horn," said the supervisor. "I assure you, we'll be very careful—"

Looking at Jerry Weber, Boo Brown said, "I'm sorry, kid. You see how it is, don't you? Got to play that concert in San Fran this afternoon, or I'd let you have both the seats. But as it is, I got to say no. I can't let them put Mama down there with all them heavy suitcases."

Weber looked hopefully at the Congressman, who shook his head slowly. "I'm sorry, son," he said. "I thought of letting you have my seat earlier. But there are too many people lined up for me to see in San Francisco, and no way to cancel them out."

"Sure," said the young soldier bitterly. "I told you the way my luck was running I'd get bumped. By a goddamned fiddle!"

He bent to pick up his suitcase.

17

"Hold on," said Boo Brown. To the supervisor: "You the man? The real man?"

"What do you mean?"

"I mean, who says what goes on aboard that big-assed bird? You? Or somebody else."

"Well, the Captain's in charge, of course—"

"Get him out here."

Shocked, the gate supervisor said, "I couldn't do that!"

"Why not?"

"Why, you just don't. Nobody calls the Captain off his plane once he's boarded."

"Could you if you had good reason?" asked Lindner.

"Yes, but—"

"Mister," said Boo Brown, reaching out with one ham-hand and squeezing the ramp supervisor's bicep until the man's shirt split, "you got a very good reason. Unless you want folks to call you Lefty from now on."

"That isn't necessary . . ." began the Congressman, but by then the supervisor had picked up his telephone.

"Captain O'Hara, report to Gate Five ticket counter, please," his voice said over the loudspeakers, echoing along the crowded corridors. Boo Brown released his arm, took out a handful of crumpled bills and stuffed them into the supervisor's pocket.

"Hell, no, man," he said over the supervisor's protests, "I owe you for a shirt."

"What's the problem?" said a sharp voice. It was O'Hara, his uniform jacket unbuttoned—for he had merely thrown it on as he left the flight deck in response to the announcement.

Lindner stepped forward, introduced himself and explained the situation. O'Hara looked from one man to another as the Congressman's voice droned on.

18

"Is this," O'Hara snapped at the gate supervisor, "why you dragged me off my plane?"

"Sir," said Jerry Weber, "if I don't get to San Francisco this morning I'm in bad trouble."

"Don't sweat it, kid," said the Captain. "Do you have a ticket?"

"Yes, sir."

"Stamp it," O'Hara told the gate supervisor. Then, to Boo Brown, "Come on, get that cello of yours on the plane. We'll find some place to put it. Get a move on. We're late already."

As the three men followed O'Hara aboard, Boo Brown said wonderingly, "That man don't fool around, does he?"

"He's the Captain," said Jerry Weber.

It was exactly 8:00 A.M.

## THE SECOND HOUR

O'Hara's right hand curled around the four throttle knobs. His left hand held the control yoke—firmly, but without gripping.

The 707 waited on the taxi strip. There were two planes ahead of it.

"If this takes much longer," muttered Sam Allen, "we're going to arrive low on FOD."

"Shhh!" O'Hara said angrily.

Each of the four Pratt and Whitney engines in the wing pods gulped kerosene fuel at an alarming rate. Compressors forced air into confined space until it became as unyielding as steel. Razor-sharp blades whirled and whined with an intensity that could have destroyed the ground crew's hearing in a matter of seconds had they not worn protective ear-caps.

In the left seat, symbol of Command, Captain Michael O'Hara squinted at the United Airlines DC-8 turning onto the runway. Heat shimmered above the blast shield as jet exhaust seared against it with the intensity of a welding torch. He was ashamed that he had allowed his temper to show itself against Sam Allen. The young First Officer was one of the best on the line, and O'Hara had told Management often that Allen would make a first-rate pilot once he advanced to the magic seniority number that marked the transition between First Officer and Captain.

O'Hara still felt uneasy about this flight. Like most airline pilots, he was an exceedingly cautious man. A maxim of his flight instructor at Kelly Field during the Second World War had stuck with him ever since: "There are old pilots, and there are bold pilots—but there are no *old, bold* pilots." O'Hara did not like the weather picture in San Francisco at all, and hovering just below the level of consciousness was the half knowledge that he had decided to continue with Flight 901 for personal reasons. His daughter's voice, when she had called from Portland at 2:00 A.M., had kept him sleepless the remainder of the night.

"Daddy," she had said, in her young-old, fifteen-trying-to-be-twenty voice, "I'm really worried about Mom."

Ashamed that he had to say the words, O'Hara said, "She's drinking again." A statement, not a question. Through the long separation and the eventual divorce, he had fought constantly to keep Jenny from becoming a pawn in her parents' hostilities. Even now, eight years later, he was still not sure how successful he had been.

"Yes," his daughter replied, "but it's worse than before. She hides the bottle and pretends she's just having a couple of beers. I hear her moaning in the middle of the night and find her passed out in the hall. Daddy, it's awful. I'm afraid."

He had told her not to worry, that he would fly up from San Francisco and see her tomorrow. Secretly he was afraid too. A doctor had once explained the progression of alcoholism to him, pointing out that when it was combined with an unstable personality such as that of his ex-wife, Joyce, the possibilities for destructive acts were magnified.

Now, moving into position at the foot of runway 180, he criticized himself silently for letting his fear for Jenny prod him into accepting responsibility for a flight that he felt was ill-advised.

Behind him, the Flight Engineer, John Bimonte, had not missed the flicker of hostility between the two pilots. Bimonte frowned. He did not like to discover traces of humanity or feet of clay in his superiors. The very qualities that made Bimonte a good subordinate demanded perfection from his leaders. Silently, uneasily, he monitored the array of pointers, dials, and blinking lights. No one spoke. Except for the whine of the powerful jet engines outside the plane, the flight deck was silent.

In the forward cabin, Hazel Martin and Angela Shaw were at their takeoff positions, strapped in at the small table that was considered the First Class Lounge. They had removed their blue uniform jackets and were soft and feminine in the yellow blouses and snug skirts that would be their working uniform across the nation.

Hazel Martin, without being obvious about it, studied the girl sitting across from her. As much as it was possible for her to like another woman, Hazel liked Angela. The younger stewardess seemed more mature and dependable than others her age. Hazel sensed the problem Angela faced with Paul Manchester, and this, too, brought her closer to the girl. Once, years ago, when she first began flying, Hazel had turned down a proposal because she did not want to abandon her career. Now she found herself proving the saying, "If a stew flies five years, she'll keep on as long as the company lets her."

As for Angela, she was considering the same question. Did she really want to risk losing Paul in exchange for the hard work, inconvenience, and poor pay of being a stewardess? What was she doing sitting here, strapped into an aluminum tube with wings, waiting at the end of a runway for the command that would hurtle her into the sky—when she could be nestled in the warmth of Paul's arms before the fireplace of Montauk cabin? Unconsciously she shook her head slowly—and Hazel Martin saw and understood.

Boo Brown was sprawled in a left-hand aisle seat in the First Class section, half of his huge bulk in the seat, the other half bulging out into the aisle. His eyes were fixed uneasily on the black, hour-glass case of his cello— wedged into the coat rack between the first class compartment and the lounge.

"Man," Boo said to the young soldier seated beside him, "I hope Mama's going to be all right up there."

Specialist Five Jerry Weber said nothing. He gripped his seat arms and stared out the window. When they first sat down, back at the terminal, he had been ebullient and profuse with his thanks to the black musician. Embarrassed, Boo Brown had told him to cool it, that he was saving three hundred bucks by getting a free ride for Mama. But now the young soldier was tense and preoccupied. Boo noticed and thought, *The kid's afraid to fly!*

Three rows back, Congressman Arne Lindner had put on his glasses and was going over the notes for his speech that morning in San Francisco. As new Chairman of the Committee on Natural Resources, Lindner was disturbed by the increasing pollution of rivers and offshore waters. He had a clean-up proposal for Oakland Bay and planned to try it on the audiences today. He glanced at his watch. Eight-fifteen. They were late getting off. He wondered if he had cut it too fine for his first meeting—and then thought of the young soldier who was worried about missing his shipment and smiled. No matter what problems we have, he thought, someone else always has worse ones.

Back in the Tourist cabin, Harriet Stevens tried once again to adjust her seat belt comfortably. Junior-to-be made it difficult. She pressed the call button and Lovejoy Welles came forward.

"I can't get this fastened," Harriet said. Lovejoy nodded and hurried up to the forward compartment where she asked Angela for one of the extension belts usually carried aboard for obese people.

"I don't know what happened to them," Angela said. "We've only got one, and he's"—indicating Boo Brown—"got it."

Lovejoy sighed. "I'll try," she said. She explained the situation to Boo, who gallantly gave up his seat belt saying, "I'm too heavy to be thrown out of this thing anyway," rushed back and helped Harriet Stevens fasten in, and returned to her own seat in the rear where she was reading *Flying High*, a book about how to be an airline stewardess. There was nothing in it about such situations.

Harriet Stevens had originally been squeezed in the middle seat between two businessmen, but seeing her difficulty, the man on the aisle seat had suggested changing places and now she had a little more room to stretch her

24

legs. The airplane felt hot and stuffy to her. No one else seemed to be bothered. She hoped she was not coming down with some sort of virus. Since becoming pregnant, Harriet had been careful not to use drugs or antibiotics and worried constantly about contracting an illness that would require them. She sighed. It seemed as if they were spending an unusually long time on the ground.

Cramped in the metal fuselage of the Boeing 707, ninety passengers and seven crew members waited for the signal from the JFK tower for the takeoff roll to begin.

And, waiting quietly among them, was the hijacker.

"Here we go," said O'Hara.

His right hand moved the throttle knobs forward slowly. Kerosene surged through the fuel lines, burst into the combustion chambers with an animal roar, ignited and flamed into white-hot gas.

"Eighty-five per cent power," intoned Sam Allen. Then, "Ninety."

"Water injection," said O'Hara.

Hundreds of gallons of distilled water poured into the engine, mixed with compressed air, and expanded into superheated steam. The compressor blades whirled faster. The jet whine seemed to tremble the ground.

"Ten thousand RPM," said Sam Allen.

O'Hara nodded. "Full forward on the yoke," he commanded.

Allen pressed his weight against the control yoke and the jet shuddered as its mighty blast beat the cool morning air into whirling heat eddies. O'Hara released the control yoke on his side of the cockpit and grasped the nose steering control wheel. The giant plane would have

25

to move in excess of a hundred miles an hour before the control surfaces would be completely effective, so until that speed he would steer the nose wheels much as a driver steers the wheels of a car. No further words were necessary. He released the pressure he had been keeping on the brakes linked with the rudder pedals and Flight 901 began to roll.

Slowly, ponderously, distressingly unhurried at first, the 707 accelerated steadily.

"Thirty seconds," reported the First Officer. "A hundred five knots."

O'Hara released the nose steering control and both hands held the yoke. His feet touched the rudder pedals delicately. They were firm and responding. The jet was still accelerating. More than half a mile of runway had already vanished behind them.

"V One!" called Sam Allen. This was the point of no return. To brake the heavy plane to a safe stop in case of an aborted takeoff, O'Hara had to initiate action now. The jet's speed registered at 150 knots.

"Rotate," said Allen.

O'Hara's hands pulled the control yoke back slowly. The plane's nose rose slowly, slightly—not more than seven degrees. But the increased angle of attack generated tremendous lift and as ground friction lessened, the jet shot forward.

"V Two!"

Liftoff!

The wheels broke contact with the runway. The silver wings flexed under the increased load they carried. Still gaining speed, the 707 rose swiftly above the airport. To the passengers, it was as if the earth fell away beneath them.

"Up gear," said O'Hara. Allen bent forward and pulled the gear lever with his left hand. There was a grinding sound, a heavy *thump!* and the plane shot forward even faster. When the air speed indicator pointed to 200 knots, O'Hara commanded, "Up flaps," and Allen obeyed.

O'Hara sighed and settled back. "Let 'em smoke," he said.

Bimonte turned off the "No Smoking" sign.

Flight 901 was on its way.

A.M.

## THE THIRD HOUR

E S T

The hijacker wondered if it was time to act, made a move to get up, then decided against it. The less time the air crew and the authorities on the ground had to react, the more chance for success.

The four stewardesses moved quickly up and down the aisles, serving breakfast to those who wanted it. In first class, the eggs and Canadian bacon were arranged on heavy plates bearing the insignia of Trans-America Airlines. In tourist, they were prepacked in heat-and-serve plastic trays.

One of the young women bent over, a Silex in her hand, and said, "More coffee?"

Drawn back from reverie, the hijacker looked up, hesitated, then said, "Yes."

The plane buffeted slightly, and the coffee overflowed from the cup the stewardess was passing.

"Oh!" she cried. "I'm sorry. Let me get a cloth—"

It was an omen for the hijacker, who said, "Never mind, I'll take care of it myself in the rest room."

Unsteadily the hijacker got up and moved carefully along the aisle.

Flight 901 was at its assigned altitude, 32,000 feet. O'Hara had adjusted the autopilot to keep the jet straight and level. The indicator showed 530 miles an hour true air speed, but with the veering head wind subtracting almost fifty miles an hour from this, actual ground speed was 480. This would increase, as fuel was consumed and the weight of the aircraft diminished—unless the head winds increased proportionately. The engine compressors had been reduced from 10,000 to 8500 RPM.

Unnecessarily, since he already knew the answer, O'Hara asked, "Fuel consumption?"

"14,000 pounds an hour," said John Bimonte.

The Flight Engineer was already hard at work on the meticulous flight record that corresponds to a ship's log, putting critical instrument readings and course changes down on paper. Aptly enough, this record is officially known as the "Howgozit Chart."

"Fuel over destination?"

"A little under, boss. I figure we'll have around 29,000 pounds on final."

O'Hara smiled. "That's close enough, Johnny," he said.

Bimonte was not soothed. "If those head winds drop a couple of knots, we'll build up a reserve," he said.

"Don't worry," said O'Hara. "We're not going to Reno today."

He was right. At that moment, the hijacker was in one

of the toilets, getting ready to let the crew of Flight 901 know where they were going.

A slim, dark-haired girl who looked vaguely like a hippie beckoned Angela Shaw over.

"Excuse me," said the dark-haired girl, "but there's something I think you ought to see."

"Oh?" said Angela, puzzled.

"In there," said the girl, pointing.

"In the rest room?"

The girl nodded. Angie repressed a sigh. This was all she needed. Someone had probably been air sick. She forced a smile, said, "Thank you," and opened the door to the toilet, prepared for the acidulous smell of vomit.

The room seemed normal. Angela looked around, puzzled, started to leave—and then stopped, shocked. She stared at the mirror disbelievingly, then stepped out into the aisle. The black-haired girl was waiting.

Her voice trembling, Angela asked, "Did you do that?"

"Me?" replied the girl. "Not on your life. I may be a little kinky, but that stuff isn't my bag."

"You stay here," said Angela. "Don't let anyone go in. And don't say a word about this."

Angela hurried forward, caught Hazel Martin's eye, and beckoned to her. Hazel came back.

"There's something in the forward john," Angela said. "That girl says she found it. I believe her."

Without a word, Hazel went inside. She reappeared in seconds.

"Young woman," she told the dark-haired girl, "this is serious. If you did it, admit it now. It'll be better all around."

"Shove it, grandma," said the girl. "I found it, I showed

30

it to you, and now you want me to take the rap. The hell with you."

She started back to her seat. "Wait," said Hazel. "What's your name?"

"Elly Brewster."

"Elly, I'm not accusing you. But you understand how important it is for us to know if this is a hoax or not."

"Since you ask me," said the girl, "I don't think it's a hoax."

"How do you know?" asked Angela.

"Because," said the girl, "I'm scared out of my skull. And hoaxes don't scare me."

"You two wait here," said Hazel. "And don't—"

"I won't let anyone in," said Angela. Hazel hurried away. Angela and the girl stood awkwardly in the aisle. Several nearby passengers looked at them curiously.

"Do you live in San Francisco, Elly?" Angela asked, just to be saying something.

The girl shook her head. "No," she said hoarsely. "My boy friend was drafted. He's shipping overseas. But not from—"

Her voice trailed off. Hazel had reappeared. With her was O'Hara, looking stern and official in his Captain's uniform. Hazel nodded at the toilet and he entered, closing the door behind him.

He was inside for what seemed a very long time. The curious passengers were talking among themselves now. When he came out again, O'Hara beckoned the three women over.

He spoke first to the girl. "Miss," he said, "the chances are good this is some kind of bad joke. I appreciate your calling it to my attention. I have to ask you not to mention it to anyone else on this plane. Unfortunately all peo-

31

ple aren't as cool-headed as you."

"Mister," said the girl, "I'm wetting my pants."

O'Hara choked slightly and covered his mouth with one hand to hide a sudden grin. "Me too," he said seriously. "But let's keep it to ourselves, all right?"

"Why not?" said the girl. He gave her shoulder a gentle shrug and she turned to go back to her seat.

In an undertone O'Hara said, "I took the place apart. There's nothing in there, unless it got flushed down the john."

Hazel Martin shook her head. "Maybe it could have with the old chemical tanks, the ones that had those rubber valves. But these new ones get stuffed up with a wad of Kotex. You'd never get a—"

He stilled her with a wave of his hand. "All right," he said. "Hazel, you come forward with me. Angie, lock this door—"

"I can't," she said. "Not from the outside."

"Tape it up with masking tape then," he said. "I don't want anyone in there. Understood?"

"Yes, sir."

"I'll send Johnny back with the tape," he said, and hurried up the aisle with Hazel, whispering to her.

The toilet door seemed to draw Angela like a beckoning specter. She opened it and stepped inside. The public address system clicked on, and Hazel's voice said, "In case you've been wondering about the gathering outside the port rest room, we've had a little flush trouble and . . . well, I'm afraid that things backed up on us and we're going to have to seal off that particular room. But there are three others aboard, so I hope you won't be inconvenienced. Thank you."

Angela stepped outside and shut the door. She closed

32

her eyes, but she could still see the words scrawled on the mirror in bright orange lipstick:

THIS IS NO JOKE! I HAVE HIDDEN A BOMB ABOARD THIS PLANE AND I CAN SET IT OFF AT ANY TIME WITH A RADIO. THIS PLANE MUST BE TAKEN TO SEATTLE, NOT SAN FRANCISCO. DO NOT TRY TO FOOL ME OR I WILL SET OFF THE BOMB. I DON'T CARE IF I DIE BECAUSE I HAVE NOTHING TO LIVE FOR ANYWAY. TAKE THIS PLANE TO SEATTLE OR ELSE.

John Bimonte, his face white, hurried back with the masking tape and Angela began to seal the toilet door.

The hijacker, who had noticed the commotion, hid behind a magazine and trembled.

# THE FOURTH HOUR

"It's a crackpot joke," said Sam Allen. "My God, no-body hijacks a plane to go to Seattle! It's ridiculous."

"I'm not too sure, Sam," said O'Hara. "I've got a gut feeling about this one. Sure, it's crazy—but what sane person commits air piracy?"

John Bimonte, who had been listening carefully, said, "How do we know this joker's really got a bomb?"

"We don't," said the Captain. "But even if there's only one chance in a thousand that he's telling the truth, those odds are still too dangerous."

"Mike . . ." began Sam Allen.

"What?"

"How do we know it's a *he?* Guys don't usually carry orange lipstick around, do they?"

"Sam," O'Hara said wearily, reaching for the radio mi-crophone, "nobody know what goes on inside a hijacker's mind. He, she, it doesn't matter. Somebody back there is all whacked up in their head, and we're going to have to play along."

"We're going to Seattle?" asked John Bimonte.

O'Hara nodded. "We're going to Seattle," he answered.

Satisfied, the Flight Engineer reached for his slide rule. There would be new fuel computations to make, course corrections to be allowed for . . . but these were finite, provable facts that he could understand.

Yawning, just ready to take ten in the men's room, Air Traffic Controller Harvey Brandt blinked at the green face of his radar scope and shrugged his shoulders to relieve the ache behind his neck. Behind him, his relief stared at the scope, "getting the picture" in Controller talk. When he slipped into Brant's chair, it would be as if all the information in Harvey's mind had mysteriously transferred itself to the new man.

"No sweat," muttered Harvey. "Trans-America 901 on JR 78 will be picking up JR 82 over Hiram. Altitude 32,000. Nothing else in that area. Some local traffic, but nothing above 14,000."

"Right," said the new man. "I've got the picture."

Harvey yawned again, straightened—ready to hand his post over to the relief man. Then he froze.

"Wait a minute!" he said tersely. Half out of his chair, he listened carefully to the voice speaking quietly into his earphone. His hand switched the radio to "Transmit" and he said, struggling to maintain calm in his voice, "Roger, Trans-America 901. I read you five by five. I will stand by for further transmission." He threw the switch to "Receive" and said, without looking around, "Pete, get on the horn to Cleveland FBI. 901's got a hijacker on board."

"There's something funny going on," said the young soldier.

Next to him, Boo Brown looked over from his copy of *Downbeat* and said, "What do you mean, funny?"

"That announcement. Why are they making such a big fuss about a stopped-up latrine?"

Boo shrugged. "Beats me. But I'm just as glad somebody else found out 'stead of this child. You know, I was on a flight to San Juan one time, that midnight special with all those women and children going home from New York, and I went back to the throne to meditate awhile. Well, all those Spanish ladies with their airsick kids had already been in there, which wouldn't have been too bad —except just as I settled down with my copy of *The Amsterdam News,* we hit a tremendous air pocket. And the top of the throne and everything inside it came bouncing back and lifted me up in the air like a ping-pong ball on top of Old Faithful." Boo shook his head. "Son, I was some fragrant cat."

"I still think there's something funny going on," said Jerry Weber, as if the black musician had not spoken at all. "Do you think they're turning the plane around? I felt something a little while ago."

"Take it easy, boy," said Boo Brown. "The sun's still on our left, so I guess we're headed West. And the engines sound all right to me so I doubt that there's any serious possibility of our crashing. Why don't you just have a little drink and let the Captain fly this airplane?"

"They're not serving drinks yet," said the young soldier.

"Shoo, don't let that worry you," said the musician. Fishing inside his tent of a jacket, Boo Brown produced a leather-sheathed flask with the motto BE PREPARED stamped in gold in its side. "This is seventy-year-old brandy," he said. "It goes down like honey. Pass me your coffee cup."

The soldier obeyed, and Boo sloshed half an inch of amber liquid into the dark remains of Weber's breakfast coffee.

"Now," said the musician, "drink that. It's good for what ails you."

Jerry Weber hesitated. "You're not supposed to drink when you're taking pills," he said.

Boo Brown's eyes narrowed. "What kind of pills?"

"Stay-awake. I've been up all night and I didn't want to fall asleep."

"I guess that's all right then," said the musician. "I've popped a little Benzedrine myself. Except you know what they say about that stuff. For every hour of sleep you lose, it takes an hour off your life."

Specialist Five Jerry Weber smiled tightly and sipped at the brandy. "That doesn't worry me any," he said softly.

"No," said Boo Brown, thinking of his own forty-three years and how fast they had gone, "you're young enough that it wouldn't."

"Are you all right?" asked Lovejoy Welles, concerned. The young trainee had been summoned to the rear of the tourist cabin by the incessant ringing of a call button. The ringer was one of the businessmen seated next to Harriet Stevens. When Lovejoy arrived, she found Harriet white-faced and obviously in pain.

"Yes," Harriet said, getting back her breath. "The little monster just decided to go for a fifty-mile hike. I'm fine now. Could I have some more coffee?"

Lovejoy went for it, and when she returned, the pregnant passenger had propped a mirror on the folding table and was applying lipstick to a face that had regained its color. Lovejoy started to make a humorous comment on the recuperative powers of makeup, but then her hand trembled and she had to set the coffee down to keep from spilling it.

Harriet Stevens' lipstick was bright orange.

"Cleveland Air Traffic, this is Trans-America Flight 901. Do you read me? Over."

"901, this is Cleveland Air Traffic. I read you five by five. Over."

"Here's our situation," said O'Hara. "We have discovered a bomb threat in one of the rest rooms. It orders us to proceed to Seattle or be destroyed. We have no way of determining whether or not the threat is a hoax, so we have decided to obey its instructions. Request immediate clearance for Seattle and weather information for the Pacific Northwest. Over."

"Roger," said Harvey Brandt, perspiring in his air-conditioned control center at Cleveland Airport. "While I'm getting those clearances, Captain, I've got the FBI on the line. Shall I patch them in to you?"

"Affirmative," said O'Hara's voice, calm and distant.

"Captain O'Hara?" said a new voice. "This is Stanley Moore. I'm FBI Regional Director out here. Air Traffic informs me you have a hijacker aboard. That's all I know. Will you fill me in? Can you talk?"

"Yes, I can talk," said O'Hara. "So far we don't know

who the hijacker is. He or she left a bomb threat scrawled in lipstick on one of the rest room mirrors. We have been instructed to proceed directly to Seattle or risk an explosion."

"Do you have any way of knowing if the threat is real?"

"Negative," said O'Hara. "We are proceeding on the assumption that it is."

"Very wise," said Moore. "Has the hijacker made any further demands?"

"Not as yet," said the Captain. "But there's a good possibility that Seattle might not be the final destination."

"Unless someone on board wanted to get to Seattle in a hell of a hurry," said the FBI man. "All right, Captain. We'll monitor your progress and will be standing by in Seattle. If you get any further information, please contact us. We'll stay linked up with Air Traffic."

"All right," said O'Hara. "But get this straight—I don't want any shoot-outs, not while I've got passengers on this plane."

"We'll try to avoid that, Captain," Moore promised. "I'm switching you back to your Traffic Controller. Good luck, sir."

Another voice came on the circuit. "Flight 901, this is Cleveland Control. I've got your clearance and weather, but first, do you want us to pass you along to Chicago and Fargo Controls, or keep this line open? Over."

"Cleveland Control, who am I talking to?"

"Harvey Brandt, sir."

"Harvey, you sound level-headed to me. What do you recommend?"

There was a pause, then Brandt said, "I think you ought to stay linked up with us, Captain. We'll pass radar coverage along to the appropriate stations, but we're already on top of your situation here and when you pass the ball along there's always a chance of fumbling it."

"My sentiments exactly, Harvey. I hope you got your beauty rest last night."

"Don't you worry about that, sir." All thought of weariness had vanished from Harvey's mind. Now his thoughts raced ahead of the jet airliner, past Chicago and into the heartland of America . . . over the plains of Nebraska and the peaks of Grand Teton in Wyoming, across the corridor of Idaho, past the Snake River and down the final glide slope to Seattle. The last hour would be rough, Harvey knew. He had already glanced at the weather report.

"Your clearance is confirmed, sir," he said. "Remain on Jet Route 82 until you reach the Rapid City Control Zone. Pick up Jet Route 90 there and proceed on into Seattle."

"I'd like to let down to 12,000," said O'Hara. "My Flight Engineer has worked out the fuel consumption, and he figures that if we start letting down now and reach 12,000 just past the Rockford intersection, we should arrive over Seattle with 9000 pounds FOD."

"That's your decision, Captain," said the Controller. "But I must advise you that the Seattle weather is deteriorating rapidly and that there is a good possibility you will be required to divert to Boise, Idaho. 9000 pounds wouldn't be enough to get you there."

"I don't think it much matters," said O'Hara. "Something tells me that our unknown friend doesn't want to go to Boise."

"Seattle?" yelped Brigadier General (Retired) Marion Hotchkiss, president of Trans-America Airlines. "They're

40

hijacking 901 to Seattle?"

Calmly Herbert Kean, his male secretary, repeated the message he had just received from Operations. Kean was used to the General's verbal pyrotechnics. A former Green Beret, Kean was seldom flustered by anything.

"Well, what are they doing?" Hotchkiss demanded.

"They're going to Seattle, General," said his secretary. "That's the sensible thing to do."

"It's an outrage!" growled the General. This was his first experience with hijacking. Secretly he had rejoiced over the embarrassment and expense suffered by Eastern and Pan Am. "Those bastards cut my throat for the Miami run back in '59," he confided to Kean one night over drinks after a long session with the CAB, "and now they can reap the whirlwind." He had laughed throatily, coughing over his smuggled Havana cigar. "Buy Miami, get Cuba free! Ha!"

Now, however, it did not seem so funny.

"Who's the Captain?" he asked.

"O'Hara, sir."

Hotchkiss snorted and coughed. "Good man. Level. Served under me in the Eighth Air Force. He won't panic."

Kean said nothing. In his own not inconsiderable experience, he had rarely heard of any airline Captain panicking, ex-B-17 pilot or not.

"What are we doing about it?" Hotchkiss asked.

"Monitoring every transmission to and from 901," said Kean. "We've got fuel trucks standing by in Seattle just in case the hijacker decides to go on from there. The FBI is putting units together in Seattle and Boise."

"Boise? Why the hell Boise?"

"Because, sir, there's only one chance in five that 901 will be able to get on the ground in Seattle. O'Hara has radioed for permission to descend to 12,000 for most of the trip. Operations has refused the request."

General Hotchkiss stiffened. "O'Hara's in command of that flight," he said. "Do you know the reason why he wants an altitude of 12,000?"

"No, sir," Kean said blandly, "but Operations feels that the fuel margin over destination would be too low to permit diversion to the alternate field in the likely event of Seattle's being closed in."

"Good for Operations," said Hotchkiss, his voice sounding oddly like the vigorous, decisive man he had been in England during the bloody years of daylight bombing. "But Operations isn't commanding 901, Captain O'Hara is. For your information, Kean, if a bomb were to explode at 32,000 feet, that aircraft would burst like a punctured balloon. At 12,000, there is some chance of survival. Radio permission to O'Hara to make his descent."

"But, General," Kean persisted, "the prediction is for one-tenth visibility in Seattle."

"Dammit!" yelled Hotchkiss, "In 1949 during the Berlin Airlift, O'Hara was landing at Tempelhof with zero visibility! Tell him to do what he thinks best. All the way."

"If you say so, sir," said Kean, leaving the room. He did not bother to go to his private telephone. He had already given permission to 901's Captain to descend to 12,000 feet. It had then only remained for the General to think it was his own idea.

Moving carefully through the cabin, apparently attending to the passengers' needs, but actually observing them closely to search for any nervousness or unusual behavior, Hazel Martin smiled her professional smile and tried to still the butterfly of fear in the pit of her stomach.

42

Earlier, she and the other stewardesses had tried to remember who had been in the rest room. In Hazel's mind, the dark-haired girl, Elly Brewster, was not above suspicion. As she moved through the cabin she sneaked glances at the girl, who sat staring out the window with an unread *Mad* magazine on her lap.

Lovejoy Welles had reported her suspicions about Harriet Stevens.

"That's crazy," Jane Burke said. "Why would a pregnant woman hijack an airplane?"

Angela Shaw was not so sure. "Why would anyone hijack a plane?" she asked. "Do you know what the fare from San Francisco to Seattle is? I looked it up. $51.45, including tax."

"She hasn't got the money," said Lovejoy Welles.

"How do you know?" Hazel's voice was sharp.

"We were talking after I sealed up the john. She had to wait until the other one was free. She said her husband's been upset because she stayed in New York so long, and wouldn't send her any money. So she hocked her wedding ring and lied to her mother. She plans to call him from San Francisco and have him wire her the price of a ticket." The young stewardess spread her hands. "But she's afraid he won't. So this might be her way of getting there."

"You shouldn't have done that, Lovejoy. When Captain O'Hara wants the passengers to know, he'll announce it himself."

"Ye gods!" said Lovejoy. "I didn't tell her anything about our mysterious lipstick writer. We were just talking."

"Did she seem curious about the commotion?" asked Jane.

"Sure. But so was everyone else close enough to see our routine. It isn't as if we were just cleaning up after some drunk, you know. We did everything but run up the small craft warnings."

"All right," Hazel said. "Let's not spend any more time on this. I want you girls to keep your eyes and ears peeled. I don't have to tell you, this is a dangerous situation. If we can pinpoint whoever it was who wrote that message, the Captain may be able to take some kind of action."

Hazel bent over a passenger in the first class section. He was a heavy-set man, twisted down trying to get something from under the seat.

"Can I help you, sir?" she asked.

He looked up sharply. It was the Congressman. What was his name? Hazel let the card file of her memory skim through the passenger list. Lindner. Congressman Arne Lindner. A VIP.

"No, thank you," he said. "I've got it." He lifted up a long canvas object that looked like a gun case. He noticed her stare. "My fishing rod," he said lightly. "I have a date with some salmon in the Columbia River."

"Oh," she said uncertainly.

He looked at her strangely. "What did you think it was?"

"Good luck with the salmon, Congressman," she said, and hurried forward.

"We're letting down to 12,000," said O'Hara. "Slow and easy. I don't want to get our unknown friend up tight."

"Mike," said John Bimonte, "I just want to remind you that our fuel consumption jumps sixty per cent at that altitude. If Seattle's socked in—"

"It won't be," said O'Hara.

No one thought of questioning him. If Michael O'Hara said that Seattle would not be socked in, God Himself would never have dreamed of sending in the fog.

Both the Trans-America officials and the FBI had been most careful to avoid leaking information of Flight 901's plight. Cleveland Air Traffic had put a hold on all outgoing telephone calls. But despite their precautions, at 10:43 A.M., New York time, the telephone on the desk of the City Editor of the New York *Call-Record* rang.

"Harper, desk," he answered.

A distant voice said, "Mr. Harper, you don't know me—"

"No, I don't," he said. "What do you want?"

"I've got a story to sell."

"Sorry," Harper growled, "we don't buy stories." He started to hang up the receiver, but the voice interrupted him.

"You'll buy this one. There's an airplane being hijacked—"

Harper lowered his voice and said, "What did you say?"

"There's an airplane being hijacked right now, and I know all about it."

"How do you know?"

"I just do."

"And I see the future in the stars. So long, buddy." But Harper did not move to hang up the telephone this time.

"I can prove it," said the voice. "Listen."

"There were static noises and then, distantly, Harper heard, "901, this is Cleveland Air Traffic. I read you five by five. Over." A pause, and, "Here's our situation," said a second voice. "We have discovered a bomb threat in one of the rest rooms. It orders us to proceed to—"

Harper strained his ears, but there was nothing more to be heard. "Where?" he demanded. "Cuba?"

"That's what I'm selling," said the original voice. "Are you interested, or shall I call the *Daily News.*"

"I'm interested!" Harper yelled. "Listen, where did you get this? Who are you? What—"

"I want five hundred dollars. In cash. Bring it with you. I've got the rest of the tape, and by the time you get here I'll probably have more. There's a great skip right now—"

"A what?" Harper demanded.

"Never mind. My name's Ackson. Claude Ackson. I live in Apartment 1-B, at 608 West 89th Street. Ring the downstairs bell four times. Got that?"

"I've got it," said Harper. "I can't come myself, but—"

"You or nobody," said the voice. "And, Mr. Harper?"

"Yeah?"

"Don't forget the money."

"All right," said O'Hara impatiently. "It's crowded in here, so let's get moving.

Hazel Martin, Lovejoy Welles, and Angela Shaw were all crowded into the tiny alcove behind the Flight Engineer's position.

"We've all got our favorite suspect," O'Hara went on. "Right?"

"Yes, sir," said Hazel Martin. "I'm worried about that man who calls himself a Congressman. Maybe he is, maybe he isn't. But he's got something in the seat with him that could easily hold a rifle. Then there's the girl who claims she found the message. A hippie. I've got my

46

eye on her."

"All right," said the Captain. "Angela?"

"That young soldier you let on board," she said. "He's very nervous. Too nervous, for my taste."

"Lovejoy?"

The trainee told him her suspicions of Harriet Stevens. "I know she's pregnant and all that," Lovejoy said, "but I'd swear that lipstick she's using is the same color as the message in the john. And she's got plenty of reason to get to Seattle."

"How do you know what color the message was?"

"I let her look," said Angela.

"Not smart," said O'Hara. "All right. Let it drop. Here's how I see it. One of you may be right. Or I might be."

"Who do you think it is?" asked Hazel.

O'Hara brushed one hand across his thinning forehead. "The big guy with the cello case," he said. "You could put one hell of a bomb in there, couldn't you?"

Since they could not agree, the crew dispersed to their posts.

It was Angela who found the crumpled ball of paper in the small galley sink. She nearly threw it into the waste disposal under the galley but then, curious, she unfolded it and read:

WHY WON'T YOU LISTEN TO ME? I ASKED YOU TO TAKE THIS AIRPLANE TO SEATTLE AND YOU PAID NO ATTENTION. IF I DON'T HEAR FROM YOU IN FIVE MINUTES, I WILL HAVE TO SET OFF THE BOMB. PLEASE DON'T MAKE ME DO IT.

**THE FIFTH HOUR**

The building at 608 West 89th Street was one of those narrow, soot-stained brownstones on an Urban Renewal block. Several buildings near it had been gutted and were in the debris-littered process of renovation.

Ken Harper paid off his taxi and hesitated in front of the building. A high stoop climbed up the front of the brownstone, to double oak doors. Beneath the stoop, behind a wrought-iron gate, was another entrance. Harper decided to try this one. He went down the half flight of stone steps and rang the bell four times.

Quickly, as if he had been waiting just inside, a slim young man opened the wooden door, unlatched the gate, and said, "Mr. Harper?"

"Right. Ackson?"

The young man nodded, thick horn-rimmed glasses flashing in the morning sun. "Come in. I got another transmission after I talked with you. Mr. Harper, this is red hot."

48

Harper followed the young man into a basement apartment, down a long corridor and through an open door into a room filled with electronic equipment.

Claude Ackson nodded at the shelves filled with radio transmitters, receivers, tape recorders, and knob-cluttered devices so exotic that Harper could not recognize them. "My ham shack," the young man said. "I've got single sideband, medium wave, even a teletype hookup. I feed everything into a variable wave length, high gain beam up on the roof. I had to slip the super twenty bucks to get permission to mount it, but it's worth every dollar."

"Good for you," said Harper, at his watch. "What I'm interested in is, do you have something that's worth five hundred dollars to me?"

Ackson indicated an Ampex tape recorder, rack-mounted in one of the walls. "It's all on there," he said. "I played you part of the first transmission. Since then I got another one." He smiled proudly at his equipment. "Ordinarily that air-to-ground stuff is pretty well limited to line of sight. But occasionally we get an effect known as 'skip' when a signal will turn up hundreds of miles away. That's what happened this morning."

"Are you in the radio business?"

"Nope. I sell suits for Barney's. Today's my day off. I was just sweeping the bands, not listening to anything in particular, when that transmission came jumping out at me. Luckily I had the tape rolling. Look, Mr. Harper, I'm not ordinarily too interested in money, but I need a new linear amplifier and with shipping a good one comes to just around five hundred dollars. Have you got it?"

Not feeling the need for further fencing, Harper handed the young man a brown envelope. Ackson glanced at the green bills inside, jammed it into his pocket.

"Thanks," he said. "Okay, you have to promise me not to reveal your source on this. It's against the law to disclose transmissions to a third party."

Harper stared. "Even when anybody with a radio can listen in?"

Ackson shrugged. "That's the law. They could yank my license and, who knows, I might even get hit with a civil suit."

"I'll keep it tight," said Harper. He looked anxiously toward the tape recorder.

"I've duped off the pertinent stuff," the young man said, handing Harper a reel of brown recording tape. "The plane involved is Trans-America Flight 901, bound for San Francisco. Someone has written a bomb threat in one of the rest rooms, ordering them to land at Seattle instead. The FBI's in the act already. The pilot's obeying the hijacker's. instructions. That was the gist of the first transmission. It's all on there. Now, here's what I picked up a little while ago."

He pressed a button and the tape recorder began to turn.

"Cleveland Operations, this is Trans-America Flight 901. Over."

Harper sat down, lit a cigar, and listened.

"901, this is Cleveland. Over."

"Harvey?"

"Yes, Captain. What's up?"

"Pass word to the FBI that we've received a second bomb threat. Whoever the hijacker is, he or she is getting nervous. I'm going to have to make some kind of announcement to the passengers to let our mysterious friend know I'm following his instructions. Meanwhile, we've commenced our descent to 12,000. My Flight Engineer tells me that the head winds are higher than anticipated. Our FOD now looks like around 7500 pounds."

There was a pause, and Harper leaned forward impatiently. Then static rasped noisily and the recording continued.

"That's bad news, Captain O'Hara," said the Controller's voice. "Predictions for Seattle now give nine-tenths probability that visibility will be well below minimums by your ETA."

"How much below minimum?"

"Three hundred feet, with patch fog bringing it down to zero at intervals."

There was another long pause. Then O'Hara said, "Is there any field within our fuel range that is likely to be open?"

"Negative."

"Then advise Seattle to be prepared for a full instrument landing."

"I've already been in touch with them, sir. Air Traffic advises me that they recommend against such an attempt. The new Mark IV ILS system is only just operational, and Seattle advises that their controllers have not acquired full proficiency on it yet."

"Goddammit!" O'Hara spat, "Get somebody over from McCord Air Force Base in Tacoma. The Air Force ought to have somebody checked out on GCA approaches."

"I'll get right on it. Is that all, sir?"

"Yeah, Harvey. Thanks."

"Don't mention it, Captain. Cleveland Control out."

Harper was leaning forward as Claude Ackson switched off the recorder. "Do you have a telephone?" asked the editor.

Ackson nodded toward a wall instrument mounted

over one of the radios. "Be my guest," he said.

As Harper dialed the *Call-Record*'s City Room, he said, half to himself, "That poor bastard."

Aboard Flight 901, there was a loud click as the loudspeakers went on.

"This is the Captain speaking," said O'Hara's voice. "You may have noticed that we have been descending. It seems we're coming into an area of weather, and we should be more comfortable at this altitude. However, I have bad news for most of you. Because of weather conditions in San Francisco, we are forced"—there was a subtle emphasis on the word—"to divert to Seattle, Washington. I'm very sorry that this is necessary, because I know it's inconvenient. There's no cause for alarm. The plane is in top-notch shape, we haven't lost any engines that I know of, and if you're mad at me, you should see my First Officer's face. It seems he's got a girl friend in Sausalito and she's waiting at the gate." A lie, but O'Hara felt the need for some note of levity. "Blame it on the weather man, and all I can say is, from here to Seattle the drinks are on me. Have a good time."

O'Hara switched off the public address system and replaced the microphone in its magnetic cradle.

"I hope that calms our friend down," he said.

"Thanks for the girl friend in Sausalito, Mike," Sam Allen growled. "I've had my eyes on Angie for the layover. You sure fixed that."

Seriously O'Hara said, "I don't think it matters, Sam. You don't really think our hijacker is going to settle for Seattle, do you? All I hope is that we can get the passengers off there."

"Goddamn head winds!" exploded John Bimonte.

"Boss, our FOD's down to 6800 pounds now. If this keeps up we'll be lucky to even *make* Seattle."

"What if I go back upstairs?" asked the Captain.

"Too late," said the Flight Engineer. "We'd burn more fuel climbing than we'd gain."

"Mike," said Sam Allen, "what if we landed at Boise without saying anything? We wouldn't have the weather problem and how would anyone know the difference?"

"The difference," Michael O'Hara said glumly, "is a large body of water known as Puget Sound."

The private telephone on the desk of Mark Goddard, News head of Amalgamated Television Corporation, rang.

He picked up the receiver. "Goddard."

"This is Smiley," said a voice. "I think I've got something."

"Shoot."

"This is worth two big ones."

"I'll be the judge of that. If it is, you'll get them. Go ahead."

"I'm calling from the Blarney Stone. I sneaked out for a quick one. We're replating the front page."

"What's the headline?"

"Mysterious Hijacker Diverts Coast-to-Coast Jet with Bomb Threat."

"Any copy yet?"

"It's down in linotype. But I've got the subhead: Trans-America's Flight 901 to San Francisco Ordered to Seattle."

"Okay, Smiley. You've got your two. As soon as you get body copy, call me again and you'll earn a bonus."

"Right," said Smiley Mansfield, chief pressman of the

New York *Call-Record,* hanging up the pay telephone. Two hundred dollars with promise of more to come. Damn! At that rate, he wouldn't mind a few more hijackings.

Elly Brewster, the slim, dark-haired girl who had discovered the bomb threat, huddled in her seat and stared out the window at the passing clouds.

"Actually," she said to her seat companion, a middle-aged salesman from Proctor and Gamble, "I don't mind going to Seattle at all. That's where I was going anyway."

"Through San Francisco? That's the roundabout way."

"Not this early in the morning. They didn't have anything leaving directly for Seattle until one in the afternoon. I was going to connect with a flight in San Francisco, and I'd have been in Seattle three hours before the other plane got in."

"Well," said the salesman, "now you'll be there even sooner."

The girl straightened, looking at him. "Yes," she repeated slowly, "now I'll be there even sooner."

"You know, boy," Boo Brown said to the young soldier, "you may just be right. There is something spooky going on."

The brandy had apparently improved Jerry Weber's morale. He smiled and said, "Just a little weather. The Captain said so."

"Screw the Captain," said Boo Brown. "I've been on enough jet planes to know that when you hit weather, you don't go under it, you go over it. He's practically got this thing on the ground. And as for San Francisco being socked in, if San Fran's gone, Seattle went first."

"I'm sorry about your concert," said the young soldier.

Boo Brown shrugged and extended the flask. "What the hell," he said, "These things happen. It ain't your fault."

In Fairbanks, Alaska, still weary from his rest of less than three hours, William Reading struggled out of bed and staggered across the room to switch off the alarm.

"Goddamn you, Hugh Thomas!" he muttered. "Damn *all* poker players to hell and back." He reeled into the kitchen, piled high with four days of dirty dishes, and lit the gas flame under yesterday's coffee. He rubbed the back of one hand over his stubble, decided not to shave. What the hell. The bears wouldn't mind. Still half-dazed, he switched on the radio and padded back toward the bathroom.

The words caught him at the door.

"Seattle . . ."

Seattle? That's where Cathy is. He rushed back into the tiny kitchen and listened to the announcer.

"This is the fifty-eighth hijacking this year," the announcer went on, "and is unique in two respects. First, no one, not even the aircraft's crew, knows just who the hijacker is. Second, instead of ordering the plane to Cuba or some other foreign airport, the hijacker has instructed the pilot to set down in Seattle. At this moment, Flight 901 has let down to 12,000 feet to minimize the damage that might be caused by an explosive decompression. Privately, authorities are concerned that any sizable bomb might still damage the aircraft so severely as to cause its destruction. And that's the 5:00 A.M. news. Stay tuned to the Voice of Fairbanks, good music and news around the clock. Now, an interlude with Mantovani."

The telephone rang. It was Reading's hunting partner, lawyer Charles Blakemore. "Bill? Charlie here."

"Morning," said Reading automatically.

"I'm just having breakfast. What say I pick you up in an hour or so? Are you ready."

Still thinking about the news report from the mainland, FBI man William Reading said, "I guess so." He hung up the phone and went back to turn off the flame under the coffee, which was boiling.

In New York City, advertising executive Paul Manchester left his office at 627 Madison Avenue for an early lunch at the Russian Tea Room. Walking down East Fifty-Seventh Street, he glanced casually at a stack of newspapers piled beside a green wooden newsstand. They were still bound up with twine, but the headline leaped out at him.

"Let me have one of those," he told the dealer, who tried to shove a previous edition at him. "No, dammit, those down there."

Muttering, the dealer cut the twine and handed Manchester a soiled copy of the *Call Record*. The advertising man dropped a dime on the counter and began reading the front page with its huge black headlines.

"Don't block the stand, bud," the dealer said. Manchester glared at him and stepped back against a store front, staring incredulously at the newspaper.

MYSTERIOUS HIJACKER

DIVERTS COAST-TO-COAST

JET WITH BOMB THREAT

56

Trans-America's Flight 901
to San Francisco Ordered
to Seattle

(Story on page 3)

His hands shaking, Paul Manchester tore open the newspaper and saw another headline filling the top of page 3.

### TAKE ME TO SEATTLE OR I'LL KILL EVERYONE ABOARD VOWS HIJACKER

(Exclusive to the Call-Record) High drama took the stage this morning 30,000 feet over Cleveland, Ohio, when an unknown hijacker left a message in a Trans-America jet clipper ordering the pilot to divert from his scheduled destination of San Francisco, California, to Seattle, Washington.

Captain Michael O'Hara, skipper of TA's Flight 901, radioed Cleveland Air Traffic Control that he was giving way to the hijacker's demands and changing course for Seattle.

Authorities, when contacted, admitted only that there have been "irregularities" in the flight, and that "all possible measures" are being taken. Privately, one FAA official voiced concern for the flight because of bad weather in the Pacific Northwest. In addition, it was believed the hijacker might change his mind and order the aircraft to another destination. "In that case," said the official, "we've got real problems. 901's fuel situation is critical already."

The flight, which left New York's John F. Kennedy International Airport at 8:00 A.M. this morning, carried 90 passengers and a crew of seven. Captain O'Hara is in command, with First Officer Samuel Allen as co-pilot and Flight Engineer John Bimonte. There are four stewardesses, all from the New York area. They are Hazel Martin, 28; Jane Burke, 22; Lovejoy Welles, 21; and Angela Shaw, 22.

There was more, but Paul Manchester did not bother to read further. With the forgotten newspaper crumpled in his hand, he hurried back to his office.

## THE SIXTH HOUR

The stewardesses were serving lunch, submerging their unspoken fear in a flurry of activity. The passengers had taken the Captain literally on his offer of "drinks for the house" and were working their way through the liquor locker. There would be no unused miniatures today for the stews to smuggle home in their purses.

"I could use a drink myself," Angie whispered to Jane Burke as the two girls worked furiously in the tiny aft galley. All semblance of separation between first class and tourist service had broken down. The stewardesses went where they were needed—and fast, because no one wanted to displease the unknown hijacker wherever he might be sitting.

Twice, the dark-haired girl who had discovered the original message caught Angie's eye and leaned forward, as if she wanted to speak to the stewardess. But there were two men in the seats between Elly Brewster and the

59

aisle, and each time she turned back to her window.

Now, as Angie and Jane worked in the galley, Elly appeared. She stepped inside and said, "Can I talk with you?"

"Sure," said Angie. She handed the drink tray to Jane Thorp. "Why don't you pass these out?"

Jane started to protest but, seeing the warning in Angie's eyes, merely nodded and left the galley.

"You haven't had a drink yet," Angie said. "How about one on the house?"

"Not for me. When I want to get high, I stick to grass." The girl looked defiantly at Angie as if to challenge, Go on, say something. Wisely Angie remained silent. "Well," Elly Brewster went on, "I got to thinking about something. Maybe it's not important, but it might be."

"What's that?" Angie asked.

"Well, most of the people on board this plane were going to San Francisco, I guess. At least, the two fellows sitting next to me are."

"So?"

The dark-haired girl looked at the blond stewardess desperately. "But *I* wasn't going to San Francisco. I mean, I hate to tell you because of what that message in the john said, but I'm really going to Seattle. Don't you see? My boy friend's shipping out from there tomorrow, and I was going to make a connection up from San Francisco because that was the fastest way to get there. There wasn't a nonstop Seattle flight until one in the afternoon.

"Well, this is working out swell for me, because now I'll get in to Seattle at least two or three hours faster than I could have going through San Francisco."

60

Angie nodded slowly. "I'm beginning to get you," she said.

"That's what I mean," said Elly Brewster, "find somebody else on this plane who wants to get to Seattle fast and you've found your hijacker."

"Mike," said Flight Engineer John Bimonte, "we're getting into a peck of trouble. Our FOD's down to 4300 pounds."

"Maybe the head winds will drop," said the Captain.

"Maybe they'll increase, too," said Bimonte. "We may just find ourselves setting down in the Wenatchee Mountains."

"Dammit, John," said Sam Allen, "lay off. We don't have any choice."

"I know that, Sam," said Bimonte, wounded. "But I've got to give Mike the straight dope."

"Don't sweat, Johnny," said the Captain. "We'll make Seattle all right. It's what happens after Seattle that worries me."

The radio crackled. "Trans-America 901? This is Cleveland Air Traffic. Do you read me? Over."

O'Hara picked up the microphone. "I read you, Harvey. What's up."

"The fit has hit the Shan, Captain," said the Controller. "I don't know how they found out, but the TV networks are broadcasting bulletins about your problem."

O'Hara cursed under his breath. Now hundreds—perhaps thousands—of relatives, friends, and acquaintances would be worried, calling TA and the newspapers. And, who knew—the very publicity of this hijacking might plant the seed in some other twisted mind. It was a self-generating cycle.

"Have they got the story straight?" he asked.

"Pretty straight," said Harvey Brandt, hundreds of miles behind them. His radio messages were being relayed by ground stations, as were O'Hara's. "I don't have to tell you the FBI is pretty hacked. They as much as accused our guys of leaking the story for pay."

"Don't worry, Harvey," said O'Hara. "I've said mean things in my day about your boys, but I know you're innocent on this one."

"For those kind words, Captain," said the Controller, "I shall buy you a drink the next time you're in Cleveland."

"You're on," said O'Hara. "Anything else?"

"All set for GCA in Seattle," said Brandt. "They've got a team from the Air Force who are all checked out on the Mark IV, and there's a B-52 shooting practice landings right now to make sure everything's operating."

"Good work," said O'Hara. "What's visibility?"

"Zero," said Harvey Brandt. "The sea gulls are walking."

"Beautiful," said the Captain. "I'll be seeing you. Out."

"Well," said Sam Allen, staring past the nose of the 707, "anyway, now we know."

"Yes," said O'Hara, tugging at one ear lobe, "now we know."

Mark Goddard, News Director of Amalgamated Television, had a conference call going to Seattle, Boise, and San Francisco.

"What do you mean we can't get a camera plane up there?" he demanded. "The Captain of 901 doesn't seem to mind that Seattle's socked in. Don't give me excuses. Just do it! I want air to air and air to ground coverage when that jet comes in. Now, you guys at the airports—I want two teams. One with handheld cameras, try to get right out there on the ramp, make a fuss, raise hell. Maybe you'll get some footage, maybe you won't. But you'll draw all the FBI heat. Second team, set up out of sight. Both sides of the runway, got that? Big Bertha zoom lenses, parabolic mikes, the whole bit. Keep shooting no matter what."

"Mark," said a voice, "I don't think you appreciate how lousy the visibility is out here. Traffic isn't even moving on the highways."

"Do it!" yelled Goddard. "Or I'll get someone who can. Okay. Any comments? Suggestions?" There was a long pause. "Goddammit, what have I got, a bunch of yes men? One of you must have a lousy idea!"

"Gruber in San Francisco, Mr. Goddard. I was just thinking—it doesn't seem logical that Seattle would be the hijacker's final destination."

"So?"

"Well, if we had a chase plane set up with cameras and so on, we could keep up with 901 wherever it's taken. Get some great air to air stuff, and of course the landings." Another pause. "Plus," he said, "of course, we'd be right on the spot for whatever else happened. I mean, who knows—"

"It'd take another 707 to do that," said Goddard. "Otherwise, 901 might outrange our chase plane."

"Yes, sir," Gruber said unhappily. "And that's expensive."

"How expensive?"

"$31,000 a day, plus overtime and landing fees."

"Do it," said the TV newsman.

Joyce O'Hara stared at the 23-inch color set in her Portland bedroom and laughed. Her daughter, Jenny, sat on the foot of the bed and stared at the picture.

"Hijacked!" the older woman choked. "Old Mr. Perfect, never late, never wrong—hijacked! Good!"

"Mama!" said the girl, "It's not funny. They say there's a bomb aboard. Daddy could be hurt."

"Not him," said the woman. "He's too mean to die."

Jenny began to cry and ran from the room. Her mother looked after the girl. "Adolescents," she said. "Thank God they grow out of it."

Alone, she reached under the bed, took up a half pint of vodka and drank it from the neck of the bottle, spilling some down her neck and between her full breasts. It was cold and she shivered. She looked after her daughter and then, suddenly, without knowing it was going to happen, started to cry too.


Senator Philip Rice, Minority Leader and close friend of the President, got through to the White House. He was connected with the Chief Executive immediately.

"Sir," he asked, "have you heard about the latest hijacking?"

"I saw a TV flash," said the President. "It's getting to be an old joke."

"This one isn't a joke," said Rice. "Arne Lindner's on that plane."

"Lindner?"

"The Chairman of your Commission on Water Pollution," Rice said shortly.

There was a pause. Then the President's voice said quietly, "I presume you've checked that out."

"Yes, sir. Arne was in New York to talk to the Foreign Press Association. Harry Joe Channing of *The New York Times* went to JFK with him and he saw Arne get on

Flight 901."

"I'll call the Director," said the President. "I understand the FBI's already on top of the situation."

"I hope they don't get too much on top of it, sir," said the Senator. "We've been lucky so far with these nuts. Let's not change our luck with Arne Lindner on board."

"I'll alert the Secret Service," said the President. "And I'll call Mrs. Lindner."

"That's kind of you, sir," said the Senator. "Even if she hasn't heard the news reports, the papers'll be out soon. Harry Joe was helpful, but he didn't see how he could sit on news this big."

"I'll get right to her," promised the President of the United States.


"Where are you shipping out to?" Boo Brown asked the young soldier.

"Okinawa," said Jerry Weber. "I put in for Japan, but I didn't get it."

"I played Japan once," said the musician. "There wasn't a chair in the whole damned country big enough for me to sit down in." He sipped at the bourbon and water the cute blond stewardess had brought earlier. "Boy, I envy you. How old are you?"

"Twenty."

"Twenty! With your whole damned life stretching ahead of you. Live it up, kid. It doesn't come around again for a second shot. See it all, drink it all, love it all. I know of what I speak."

"I don't know," said Weber. "I try my best, you know, but I always seem to get into trouble. Back at Dix, I got a Special Court-martial for slugging a drill instructor. But I had to. I was trying to explain why I was late, and he wouldn't listen. That's what's wrong with people, they don't listen. If they'd only listen, everything would be all right. And when I was instructing heavy weapons down in South Carolina. Well, the purpose of heavy weapons is to shoot them, right? And just because a couple of rounds overshot the range and hit in some redneck's field, they shipped me out. I had to go to the Inspector General's office to get my furlough—the first sergeant wouldn't listen, I told him I couldn't go overseas without seeing my father and all he said was that wasn't his problem. I could tell he was just waiting for me to miss that shipment out of Seattle. He made it hard for me to get there, they didn't pay me all the furlough money they were supposed to, I was supposed to get a flight out of Stewart on MATS and they canceled the plane on me. I mean, when they're down on you, you can't do anything right."

The young soldier fumbled in his pocket and took out a folded set of travel orders, thrust them toward Boo Brown. "Look at these orders. 'EM will proceed at his own expense to Port of Embarkation, Seattle Washington, reporting not later than 0900 November 11.' At my own expense! Just because I wanted to go home first and didn't take their lousy military transportation. Besides, I tried at Stewart. It wasn't my fault they canceled the flight. That lousy first sergeant must have had a lot of pull, to get a MATS flight canceled. And he had the Brooklyn police tuned in on me, too. I mean, I'm twenty years old, I can drink in New York legally. But the cops put the pressure on the bartenders, and even with my Permanent Class A Pass and my leave papers, they'd give me a hard time about buying a beer and one wouldn't serve me, not even after I brought my father down to straighten him out. That's what I mean, they just don't listen. When I'm President, I'm going to pass a law to make them listen. Like, take these stewardesses on this airplane. Do you think they listen? I asked for more coffee half an hour ago. You heard me. Black coffee. But no, that Captain up front makes a big deal out of going to Seattle, and now it's like we're back in some Brooklyn bar. I can't get what I ask for. Why won't they listen to me? What's so special about going to Seattle? It's just a Port of Embarkation. I'll be late, but I'll still make the shipment, so they can't bust me. Do you know if you're in the lower three grades, you still have to pull KP? On Okinawa, with all those gooks, you still have to pull pots and pans or the clipper? I like Dining Room Orderly myself, I always got up early and put in for that job because you get a nice break after breakfast and another one in the afternoon. But if I keep my stripes I won't have to pull KP at all out there. It'd give that first sergeant a big kick if I got busted, that's what he's got in mind. I told my father all about him, and he said if I got in any trouble he would go down to South Carolina and beat him up, but I don't trust that first sergeant, he'd probably take out a .45 and shoot my father, so I told my father that we were buddies except I was lying. Anyway, I'm going to make the shipment, and I bet they won't even be mad at me, because they treat people real nice who get hijacked. I just wish I could get some more coffee, because that brandy made me awful thirsty."

Boo Brown, who had listened patiently at first, then with a growing sense of apprehension, and finally with anxious concern, said, "Listen, kid, my back teeth are floating. Let me hit the head, and then I'll see that the stewardess gets you some more coffee. Okay?"

"Make her listen," said the young soldier.

"I will," said the musician, climbing awkwardly out of the seat.

Air Force Captain Robert Grundig leaned over the shoulder of Master Sergeant Benjamin Puzo and said, "He's a little low."

"Yes, sir," said Ben Puzo. "But there's a hell of an up bump just outside the outer marker. It'll balloon him back on the glide path."

Just then, to verify his words, the bright pip on the radar screen changed position. "See?" said Ben. "He bounced up a good fifty feet." he bent his mouth down to the microphone and said, "That's it, Air Force 301. You're right on the glide slope. Speed a little high. Three hundred yards to touchdown. Maintain your current rate of descent. A little right rudder—the ground wind's picking up. That's fine. Now start your flareout. Report in when you make visual contact. Okay, get your nose up. Fifty feet, forty, thirty—"

"Sergeant," said a voice over the radio, "this is Air Force 301. I beg to report that we're on the ground, but I still haven't seen it yet. Over."

Ben Puzo laughed. "That's the way it's been all morning, sir," he told Grundig. "We're getting them down all right, but they don't know where they've been or where they're going."

"We've still got an hour or so," said the Captain. "Let's shoot a few more. From what I hear of that civilian aircraft's fuel situation, they're only going to get one try."

"We'll make it a good one, sir," said Ben Puzo. He meant it. Ben was at home with the electronic signals of the Ground Controlled Approach equipment as he would have been in his own electric kitchen. "Air Force 301, are you still on the runway?"

"Ground Control, this is Air Force 301. I think so. At least we haven't seen any Avis signs."

"Get ready to go around again," said Puzo. "It's flight pay time."

"What do you mean, cancel your Caracas trip?" asked Harold Brooks, president of Brooks and Mailer. "It's all set up. Alberto is expecting you tonight."

"Angie's plane has been hijacked," Paul Manchester said. "I'm flying to Seattle."

"Paul, I'm sorry," said Brooks. "Is she on that San Francisco flight?" Paul nodded. Brooks went on, "But what good can you do? Listen, you know what a problem we've got down there. Those Cariocas are going to lose the Antilles Oil account. That's the last big one left, since the nationalization. Without it, the office could go under."

"Let it go," said Paul Manchester. "Do you want my resignation?"

Harold Brooks stared. "Of course not!" he sputtered. "But have a little perspective."

"I'm just getting some," said Manchester. "I'm starting to realize what's really important and what isn't. Look, postpone the trip for a week. Tell them to stall. Tell Alberto to come down with amoeba. I'll make the trip Monday."

"All right," said Brooks. "I'll see what I can do. But be careful."

"Don't worry about me," said Manchester. "I'm not the one who's been hijacked."

"Look at him, with that thing," Jane Burke whispered to Lovejoy Welles.

Drowsing in his seat, Congressman Arne Lindner held

the canvas case in his lap, playing idly with the zipper that ran its brown length.

There came an incessant dinging of a call button. The girls looked around. None of the indicator lights were lit.

"I think it's in the forward john," said Lovejoy.

"Oh-oh," said Jane. "Somebody's sick. It's your baby, Lovejoy. Rank hath its privileges."

Lovejoy grimaced, but made her way forward. One of the two lounges had a light on the door that shadowed the word "Occupied." She tapped at the door. Inside, the slide lock was pushed aside and the door opened a crack. Lovejoy peered in, the words "Excuse me" already leaving her lips—and almost screamed.

A giant black man sat on the closed lid of the toilet. He pressed one pudgy finger against his lips.

"Miss," he whispered, "I got to see the Captain. Don't make no fuss. Just get him back here. Can you do that?"

Backing away, Lovejoy bobbed her head. "Yes, sir, I can," she said. "Only don't do anything desperate."

"Don't you worry about this child," he said. "I just want to see the Man. Tell him it's important."

"I will," she promised and hurried forward.

A moment later the Captain stolled back casually. He tapped on the rest room door. "It's open," said a voice. O'Hara went inside. The tiny room was barely large enough for the two men.

"I understand you wanted to see me," O'Hara said, looking down at Boo Brown. It had not surprised him at all to be told that the black musician was waiting.

"I sure do, Captain," said Boo Brown. "Listen, man, this plane is being hijacked."

"I wondered when you'd get around to telling me face to face," said O'Hara.

70

Boo Brown stared at him. "What are you talking about, man?" he demanded. "I just now found out, and I thought I'd better let you know."

O'Hara frowned. "We're going to Seattle," he said. "I announced it over the loudspeaker. Isn't that what you wanted?"

"Me? Me wanted? Man, you're on the pipe. I just wanted to tell you I figured out we're being lifted, and I think I know who's doing it. I just wanted to ask you if you needed any help."

My God! thought Michael O'Hara, I've been wrong again. Aloud he said, "You're right, Mr. Brown. We have received two threats to bomb us unless we proceed to Seattle."

"It's that kid soldier sitting next to me," said Boo Brown. "He's been nervous as a cat all morning. Then, just a while ago, he went into a soliloquy that ran longer than *Hamlet*. The whole world's down on him, he has to make his shipment or get in real trouble. You know the bit. We both got it at the loading gate. But what he didn't tell us there was—his shipment's not in San Francisco, it's in Seattle. Do you dig the picture, man? He's nabbed this whole airplane to try and make that shipment from Seattle."

"Why are you so sure?"

"He dropped it a while ago. He said something about how he probably wouldn't get dinged at all for being late, because they're nice to people who get hijacked." The musician sucked in his breath. "Do you think he's really got a bomb?"

"I don't know," said the Captain. "You've spent the morning with him. What do you think?"

"He might have. He's got heavy weapons experience.

71

And, man, he's all loose inside his head. That kid's a Section Eight."

O'Hara made his decision. Boo Brown's story had convinced him. "All right," said the Captain. "We don't want him to know anyone's caught on to him. Let him say anything he wants, don't argue. Maybe he'll just get off in Seattle with the rest of the passengers. That's what he wants to do—let's help him to do it. It's the safest thing for everybody. Do you understand what I'm saying?"

"Captain," said Boo Brown, "I read you loud and clear."

P.M.

**THE SEVENTH HOUR**          E S T

"Any word from them?" Captain Robert Grundig asked nervously.

"Relax, Captain," said Master Sergeant Ben Puzo. "We're in good shape. We'll grease those civilians onto the runway like butter on a biscuit."

"That last landing was kind of rough," the Captain persisted.

"Not under these conditions, sir," said Puzo. "I've seen them drop in from three times that height under VFR and nobody complained."

"Jesus," muttered Grundig, "I could have joined the Navy. My father wanted me to join the Navy. Do you know what will happen to us if we goof this one? Puzo, there is an experimental base on the floating pack ice that makes Thule look like Miami Beach. That's where they'll send us."

"Maybe that's where they'll send you, Captain," Puzo

73

said, with a grin, "but as for this boy, he ain't making no mistakes today. Listen, sir, how about some coffee?" As he spoke, the sergeant started to rise from his chair in front of the light-flickered console.

"Stay put, Puzo," Grundig said, hurrying toward the door. "I'll get it. You relax."

Leaning back in the chair, Master Sergeant Benjamin Puzo yawned and said, "Yes, sir!"


The rented Boeing 707 was circling Seattle at 23,000 feet. Beneath that altitude, cloud cover shrouded the land far below.

Allen Ross, the only Amalgamated Television Corporation announcer at a nearby open weather airfield had been rushed from the Boise, Idaho, ATC station, hurried aboard a rented jet airplane along with two cameramen and a sound man—which stripped the Boise station of technical personnel—and was now surveying the clouds below with a gloomy face.

"I don't like this," he commented unnecessarily. "Are we supposed to go down into that soup? Do you know what happens to planes flying around at 350 miles an hour in fog? When they can't see one another? Goddard's out of his skull."

George "Happy" Gunther, the station's number one cameraman, fiddled with the zoom lens on his movie camera. "We'd be wasting our time," he said. "You can't see, let alone film, in fog."

"No," said Ross, "we don't have a chance in hell of getting anything, but if we don't try we're in crap city. Goddard wants coverage," he grumbled. "And he'll can our asses if we don't get him some film."

74

"You can't shoot what you don't see," the cameraman said.

In Portland, Joyce O'Hara stumbled out of her bedroom, a growing sense of fear trembling her face.

"Jenny?" she called. "Honey, where are you?"

There was no answer. Joyce realized suddenly that the apartment had been deathly quiet for over an hour. She stumbled over a hassock, kicked it aside in a frenzied spasm of anger.

"I'll whip you!" she shouted. "This is no time for tricks. Come out, Jenny!"

But there was no answer. She blundered into the kitchen. Her throat was parched. Maybe there was a cold beer left in the refrigerator. She reached for the handle and then saw the note, propped up against the toaster.

Her hand shaking, Joyce O'Hara lifted the folded sheet of paper and read:

> Mama, Jeff is going to fly me to Seattle. He thinks he can make it without too much trouble. Don't worry, he got his instrument rating last month and he's been practicing every time he got a chance. We're taking his father's Piper Cherokee. It's fully instrumented with ILS and everything and we ought to be in Seattle in just over an hour. I don't know why, but I just have to be there when Daddy lands. I'll telephone you. Love,
>
> Jenny

Joyce O'Hara began to cry again as she crumpled the note. Jeff was a twenty-year-old boy Jenny had met at the airfield a few months before, when she persuaded Joyce to let her begin flying lessons. He was so young, Joyce thought . . . they were both so young.

She rushed to the telephone hanging near the sink, yanked it off its hook and reached for the dial. Then she hesitated.

Slowly she replaced the instrument. There was no one to call. No one.

She opened the refrigerator and reached for a can of Olympia Beer.

"Mike," said Flight Engineer John Bimonte, "this is our last chance to divert to Boise. I just checked the tower there, and they've got good visibility. But our FOD is still dropping. If we don't divert within another five minutes, we're committed to Seattle."

"Johnny," O'Hara said softly, "we're committed to Seattle in all events."

On his return to the flight deck, he had conveyed Boo Brown's suspicions to the other two crew members.

"That kid soldier?" Sam Allen said, disbelievingly. "What is he, some kind of nut? Didn't he ever hear of the telephone? If he was going to be late he could have called his C.O. Are you sure you trust this Boo guy? He looks kind of flakey to me. Maybe—"

"It's the kid," O'Hara said grimly. "It all fits. He's got a persecution complex. His antennae are stuck out ten feet. I don't want you guys going back there. I'm not going myself. I hated to let that musician go, but the kid'd be even more suspicious if he didn't show up. A guy like him can smell things. One glance, one wrong word, and he'll know we're on to him."

"He's only one man," said Sam. "We could drop him

with the old mousetrap. You hit him high and I'll hit him low."

"And he pushes that button in his pocket and sets off his bomb."

Sam shook his head violently. "He's bluffing," he said. "He doesn't have any bomb. Do you know how sophisticated radio control is? What would he be doing with one?"

"Yeah," Captain Michael O'Hara said, "I know how sophisticated radio control is. Half a dozen ten-year-old kids near my apartment use it for flying their model airplanes."

Sam fell silent. O'Hara refused to let him off the hook. "How about it, Sam?" said the Captain. "Do you want to take the risk that this character doesn't have access to something ten-year-old kids use?"

After a long while, Sam Allen lowered his head and whispered, "No."


"I'm sorry, sir," Paul Manchester's secretary said, "I've called every airline twice. They simply can't guarantee takeoff for any flight destined for the Pacific Northwest. Weather—"

"I know about the weather," Manchester growled. "Okay. Get me Colonel Harley Davis at Air Force Public Relations down on Park Avenue."

As she dialed, his secretary said, "It's lunch time, Mr. Manchester, and—"

"I know what time it is," he barked. Then, "Sorry, Joan. I'm all keyed up."

"It's all right," she said. After a moment, into the phone: "Hello? Paul Manchester is calling Colonel Davis. Is he—He is? Just a minute." She covered the receiver with her hand. "He's there, but he's in conference. Is—"

"It's important," he said.

"It's very important," she said into the instrument. "Yes, I'll wait." She handed the telephone to Paul. "He'll be right on."

"Thanks," he said. "Listen, you go to lunch. Take the rest of the day off. I won't be back myself for a couple of days."

"But—" she began.

"Out, out, out!" he commanded, regaining some of his good humor. She gave him a smile and left. He waited.

"Hello?" said a man's voice. "Paul?"

"Yeah, Harley. Listen, are you still looking for an advertising agency?"

There was a pause, then the officer said, "Yes, but I already know how you feel, and frankly, I don't blame you. There wouldn't be any profit for you on our account. We spread too few bucks around too many media and most of it is freebies anyway."

"Forget that," said Manchester. "I need a favor. A big one. And I expect to pay for it."

"What kind of favor?" Davis asked cautiously.

"I've got to get to Seattle right now," said Manchester. "You guys must have something headed out that way. Get me on board and you've got yourself an agency."

The Colonel's voice, when it came, was low and serious. "Paul . . . is your girl on that hijacked flight?"

"Yeah. Can you do anything?"

"I'll sure in hell try," said Davis. "But you don't have to pay me off for helping. Hell, you're ex-Air Force. You could probably get on a flight just by talking to the Operations Officer."

"I don't have time," said Manchester, "and that's exactly why I will handle your account . . . because you'd come through for me without any payoff. How about it, buddy?"

"You're at the office?"

"Yeah."

"Stick right there. I've got to make a few calls. I'll get right back to you."

"Thanks," said Paul Manchester.

"I must be nuts," Angela Shaw told Hazel Martin. The two stewardesses were mixing more drinks in the forward galley.

"What do you mean?"

"I had a proposal last night. From a great guy, looks, money, everything a girl could want. So what did I do?"

"You turned him down to keep flying."

Angie bobbed her head. "That's me. The original dumb bunny. Wow, what a cluck I was. Let me tell you, Hazel, next time . . ."

The older stewardess said nothing. She lowered her head and suddenly, without warning, began to cry.

Shocked, Angie touched Hazel's cheek. "What is it?" she asked. "What did I say?"

Hazel shook her head. Sniffling, she breathed raggedly and said, "Nothing Angie. You didn't say anything. It's just me. I'm scared silly."

"You?" Angie tried to laugh. It came out sounding like a croak. "Look, it's some crackpot joke. There's nothing to get upset over. Don't you realize what this means? We're all going to get our pictures in the paper. Coast to coast. Who knows . . . movie offers. Strangers writing asking for our fair hands in marriage. Fame, fortune . . ."

"Angie," said Hazel, still choking down her tears,

79

"make me a promise."

"Anything," said the girl.

"If—when this is over, go back to your guy. Don't let him get away. Believe me, you don't get that many chances. Will you do that for me?"

"Yes," Angela Shaw said slowly, "I'll do that. But not for you. For me."

"Goddammit!" roared Marion Hotchkiss, "They're turning it into a Roman holiday. What the hell do they think's happening up there? Some kind of free show to sell soap and newspapers?"

Calmly his secretary, Herbert Kean, said, "It's a slow news day, sir. Too bad the Russians didn't decide to invade Hungary again, or—"

"Herbert," the president of Trans-America Airlines said grimly, "if you think you're being funny . . ."

"Sorry, General," said Kean. "I just don't think you ought to get personally upset this way. Your heart—"

"My heart will outlast yours, you Ivy League phony!"

"NYU isn't Ivy," Kean said, smiling. "And you knew I was a phony when you hired me. That was why you hired me."

Hotchkiss sputtered unconvincingly and rolled his brandy glass between the palms of his hands. In a more conversational tone he said, "Did I make a mistake, Herbert? The reports aren't good. The fog's worse, and I understand the fuel over destination is becoming critical."

"All true," said his male secretary. "But you made the best assessment possible under the circumstances and took the proper response to that assessment. If things go wrong it will be because things eventually always go wrong with those who break the surly bonds of earth."

80

"Surly bonds of earth?" yelled Hotchkiss. "Dammit, Kean, who the hell do you think you are? Arthur Hailey? Surly bonds of earth my ass! We're in a business, not some kind of mystic pioneering crusade. Men against the sky! Night flights to Valhalla! All bosh. Dollars and cents, they're all that interest me. Just you remember that."

"I will, General, I will indeed," promised Herbert Kean, grinning.

"We ought to be in pretty soon, huh?" the young soldier asked Boo Brown.

The black musician yawned and stretched. "I hope so," he said. "They just didn't build these seats for me. You know, man, I tried to get into a Volkswagen one time and that little mother took one look at me and melted down to a heap of scrap metal." He paused. Specialist Five Jerry Weber did not react. Boo went on, "You got any idea where they're shipping you? Overseas, I mean?"

Weber appeared not to hear him. Boo waited, crossed his hands over his ample stomach and pretended to sleep. Then, long after he had expected an answer, the young soldier said, "I told you before. Okinawa. Don't you listen?"

"I forgot," Boo said quickly. "Man, I've been hitting this juice pretty hard, you know. That's right, Okinawa. I remember now."

"You didn't listen," the soldier said accusingly. "I thought you were one of the guys who'd listen. But you're not. You're just like all the rest."

Boo decided to change the subject, but at that moment the plane plunged into a dirty gray bank of clouds and in seconds a gloomy shadow had darkened the wing surfaces. "Boy," said Boo, "if the weather's this bad up here, imagine what it must be like in San Francisco. Me, I'm just as glad we decided to go into Seattle."

"You don't know much," said Weber. "You talk a lot, but you don't know much at all. That's what you get for not listening."

"They pay me for my good looks, not my brains," Boo said desperately. "Listen, kid, how long are you going to be in Seattle before you ship? Do you have time to drag a few of the night spots with me? I hate to drink by myself."

"You drink too much," the soldier told him.

"I sure do," Boo Brown said, settling back in his seat unhappily. He wished fervently that he had decided to take the train. Except, he thought, with my luck, Jesse James would have nabbed us cold crossing Kansas.

"What did you say?" asked Jerry Weber sharply.

"Nothing," Boo said carefully. "I was just daydreaming."

"Okay," said Weber. Boo studied him and said nothing, gunshy. "I said okay," Weber repeated.

"Okay what?"

"Okay I'll have some drinks with you. That's what you wanted, isn't it?"

Boo nodded, afraid to speak and break the spell. "I mean," Weber went on, "you're not such a bad guy. I'm sorry I made that crack about you not listening. Maybe I didn't even say what I thought I said. I've been having trouble remembering things lately."

"That's all right," Boo Brown said miserably, trying to project heartiness and friendship.

Elly Brewster fumbled in her purse for a package of Kents. When she found it, she took out half a dozen ciga-

82

rettes before she selected the one she wanted. Although at first glance it seemed to be identical to the others, a careful examination would have revealed that the "tobacco" was a pale green, filled with tiny stems and dark particles. She struck a match and touched it to the end of the cigarette, then inhaled deeply. Elly held her breath for several seconds, exhaled noisily and repeated the action. The man seated next to her looked around sharply.

It smelled as if someone were burning alfalfa, he thought.

"What do you mean, you're not going?" lawyer Charles Blakemore demanded of the young FBI agent in Fairbanks.

"I had a call from the District Director," said William Reading. "He's put all of us on standby."

The lawyer laughed mirthlessly. "That's efficiency for you," he said. "Some nut hijacks a plane in Seattle, so the Alaska District is put on alert."

"You never know what will happen," Reading said.

"I know what is going to happen," Blakemore said. "I am going to go out this morning and shoot me a big goddamned bear and while you are sitting around here waiting for a telephone call from your scoutmaster, I am then going to get drunk in celebration. How do you like them apples?"

"Not very well," Reading admitted enviously.

"We ought to turn back," Jeff McGuire told Jenny O'Hara. "Dad's been having some trouble with the radio, but it checked out before takeoff and I thought he'd gotten it fixed. Now it's out but good."

"What do we need the radio for?" asked the girl. "Your

ADF is working, isn't it? We're not going to get lost."

"No, but I can't call in for landing clearance. I could get a suspension for that."

"Why? The radio went bad after takeoff, didn't it?"

"Yeah, but—"

"Well, we've got to land somewhere, and we're closer to Seattle than Portland. Besides, who knows what's happened to the weather in Portland? It might be even worse than it is up here."

Unconvinced, but determined not to back down with the girl watching, Jeff said, "Okay, but you've got to tell them the radio went out after we took off."

"I will," promised Jenny O'Hara.

"Flight 901, do you read me?" called Harvey Brandt from Cleveland Control. Static hashed his earphones and he called a second time before the answer came.

"Yeah, Harvey. This is O'Hara. Over."

"How are you doing on fuel?"

"Lousy," said O'Hara, "but we'll make it. What's new back there?"

"Would you believe that ATC has hired a charter 707 to take pictures from the air? They're orbiting Seattle, waiting for you."

"Like hell they are!" yelled O'Hara. "What do you think that nut back there is going to do if he sees another plane moving in on us? Get rid of them!"

"We're trying," said Brandt. "It's a sticky situation. They're press, and nobody wants to take the responsibility for ordering them out of the sky."

"I don't care if they're Christ Almighty, don't those idiots realize we've got an unstable individual aboard this plane? It might be just the thing to set him off."

"I read you loud and clear," said the Controller. "My chief is talking with Washington now, but there's no way of knowing if he's going to be able to call them off or not. I thought I'd warn you. Maybe you can stay in cloud cover so your guy can't see them."

"Maybe," growled O'Hara. "And maybe I can sprout wings and become an eagle, too. Okay, Harvey. Thanks."

"Nobody likes the guy who brings bad news," Harvey Brandt said softly.

"Don't sweat it, Harvey. We'll still have that drink. 901 out."

"Out," Brandt repeated.

Every soldier who has fired a .45 pistol on the range or in combat knows the flat sound the weapon makes, the slam of its recoil, the splat of the bullet smashing into its target, paper or human. The muzzle velocity of the .45 slug is in excess of five hundred miles an hour, or almost a mile—5280 feet—every ten seconds.

As thousands of people on the ground, other hundreds in the air, and ninety-seven aboard the plane itself, all strangers—yet together in this unexpected drama—waited, Flight 901 sped toward Seattle faster than a bullet leaves the muzzle of a .45 pistol.

## THE EIGHTH HOUR
(The First Half)

"All right, Paul," said Colonel Harley Davis. "Get your tail out to MacArthur Field on the double. You're in luck. There's a Vindicator fighter-bomber due to take off in thirty minutes. Report to Hangar Nine, ask for Captain Roland Lewis. He's the pilot."

"What's his destination?" Paul Manchester asked.

"Target of opportunity," said Davis. "He can take you as far as Seattle, though. From there on it's hard to tell where he might be going."

"How long does it take a Vindicator to go coast to coast?" Paul asked.

"An hour and a half, give or take a couple of minutes," said Colonel Davis. "They generally cruise around Mach Two."

"I'm on my way," said Manchester.

"That's it," said John Bimonte. "We just hit the Point of No Return. From here on in it's Seattle all the way."

Captain Michael O'Hara said nothing. Privately, the Flight Engineer's preoccupation with diverting to Boise was rasping his nerves. Although the autopilot was flying the plane, O'Hara rested his hands on the control yoke, felt tiny movements as a mechanical complex of electronics and servo mechanisms adjusted the ship's trim, its elevator and aileron movements. "What's our FOD?" he asked casually.

"Critical," said Bimonte. "I give us less than two thousand pounds now. Those head winds out there are murder."

It was just a figure of speech, but even as he heard the words leave his mouth, the Flight Engineer became aware of how literally what he had said might come to pass.

A hundred miles ahead, Seattle International Airport prepared for 901's arrival.

Four television cameramen made themselves conspicuous in the TA loading area. Two others took up positions atop the TA building, concealing themselves and their equipment.

FBI agents moved casually around the terminal. Some wore ordinary civilian dress. Others were decked out in rain gear bearing the red and yellow insignia of Trans-America Airlines. Several had taken charge of vehicles on the hardstand—jeeps and pickup trucks, even the food caterer's van.

A Shell Oil fuel truck was waiting a hundred yards from the terminal. It had been summoned in answer to a telephone call from General Hotchkiss. "What," demanded the General, "are you going to do if that hijacker wants to go on from Seattle?"

"He won't be able to," the TA regional manager replied

with some satisfaction. "901's out of fuel."

Hotchkiss discussed the manager's ancestry with some fervor. "He's a nut!" the General shouted. "Nobody can predict what he'll want. But I'll tell you what I don't want. I don't want our aircraft blown up, not even on the hardstand. Do you get my meaning? Have fuel and supplies and anything else they might need if that flight is taken elsewhere. And pass the word to the goddamned FBI, no interference! They can have him if and when he gets off that airplane. Until then, the responsibility is mine and O'Hara's. Do you read me?"

The regional manager read him. The trouble was, he knew how effectively the FBI had set up their forces, despite his pleas for them to leave the matter to the airline. He shook his head. He would try again. Meanwhile, the fuel truck was summoned, as were the caterers. "Plenty of liquor," the manager urged. "We hope he'll let the passengers off, but if he doesn't, the only thing that will keep them quiet is booze."

Now, with the fog rolling in from Puget Sound, the great airport sat quietly in its white, chilly blanket and waited for Flight 901 to arrive.

"They're on our big screen," said Master Sergeant Ben Puzo. "I figure they're around eighty miles out."

The quiet Operations Room sat tensely under its green and red lights. Eighty miles and 10,000 feet in altitude away, O'Hara lifted his microphone and said, "Harvey, do you read me?"

"Loud and clear," said Harvey Brandt, back in Cleveland.

"I'm switching over to Seattle Control now," said 901's Captain. "Thanks much for all you did."

88

"Don't mention it, Captain," said the Controller. "Let's have that drink soon."

"It's a deal," said O'Hara. "901 out." He nodded his head, and Sam Allen switched frequencies. "Seattle Tower, this is Trans-America 901."

"901, this is Seattle Tower," said a voice. "You're coming in just fine. I'm going to turn you over to a team of Air Force GCA experts who will talk you down. I believe this move was explained to you earlier. Over."

"Affirmative," said O'Hara. "Okay, Air Force. Are you on the line?"

"Yes, sir," said a new voice. "Sergeant Ben Puzo, Captain. Trust your soul to God, because your ass is mine." O'Hara choked with laughter and heard a voice in the radio background complaining, "Sergeant, that's against regulations." O'Hara broke in with, "Sergeant Puzo, I accept your offer. Screw the regulations." The other voice fell silent, and Puzo came back slowly, "All right, sir, we have you at 9000, rate of descent 500 feet a minute. Is your glide slope and ILS reading consistent with mine? I have you two degrees off course to the left and 600 feet high."

Both O'Hara and Sam Allen rechecked their instruments. Behind them, John Bimonte made rapid calculations.

"You're just about right, Sergeant," said O'Hara. "I thought I'd keep that extra altitude just in case. I don't trust the indicated heights of some of these peaks around here."   -

"No sweat, sir," said Puzo. "You're in fat city. Listen, give me an S-turn and straighten out on five-niner. I want to calibrate your rate of turn."

O'Hara disengaged the autopilot and made the requested maneuver. "How was that?" he asked.

"Five oh," said Puzo. "Okay, how's your fuel situation? Do you want to make a couple of passes for practice or come straight in?"

"We're practically sucking air," Bimonte said rapidly. "We'd better go right in."

"I don't think we can make two passes," said O'Hara. "Why don't we do it right the first time?"

"Less work for mother," agreed the sergeant. "All right, Captain, continue your rate of descent at 600 feet a minute, keep that heading, line up your needles unless I tell you otherwise. Do not acknowledge any more of my transmissions unless you have a question. Very nice, Captain, if you ever want to earn an honest living I think you can find a home flying cargo in the Air Force. Watch that rate of descent, you'll find some bad down currents around 6200 feet. Keep it on the glide slope, your instruments are smarter than both of us."

As Captain Bob Grundig stood behind him, actually holding his breath, the pudgy sergeant's voice droned on in the quiet room, joking, cajoling, wheedling . . . slowly guiding the distant airplane toward its rendezvous with the hard, unyielding earth.

"I think we're on course," said Jeff McGuire. "At least, the ILS says we are."

Outside the Piper Cherokee, the wind buffeted patches of cloud and fog past the flexing wings. Jenny O'Hara had been fighting for twenty minutes to keep from getting airsick. Now her fear conquered her stomach and she strained against the seat belt and peered out into the gloom around them.

90

"I thought I saw a mountain down there," she said uneasily.

"We should have passed over the range station by now," the boy said, ignoring the vision that swept through his mind, of mountain peaks and shattered, burning wreckage. "I think we're coming up on it. Look—the needles are starting to swing."

As the tiny aircraft approached the powerful radio antennae, needles quivered, whirled briefly, and reversed their position.

"Hey!" yelled Jeff McGuire. "That's it. We must have had a little head wind. We're right on course. We'll be on the ground in five minutes."

Weakly Jenny said, "I wish we could radio ahead for clearance." By now she had almost forgotten that it had been her urging that caused Jeff to continue the flight without an operating radio.

"We'll just go straight in," said Jeff. "They'll pick us up on their radar and vector any other traffic around us. When we don't answer, they'll catch on our radio is out."

"What the hell's that?" barked Ben Puzo, as the second blip came onto his radar scope. "Hey, one of you guys get on the horn and find out what that traffic is!"

One of the regular Controllers began speaking urgently into his microphone. "Unidentified aircraft on Course Six-oh, come in. Unidentified aircraft, break off your approach, you are entering a traffic pattern." He kept talking, but received no answer.

Now, on Ben's radar, the two blips began to converge. "O'Hara!" the sergeant said, "You're going to have to go around again. We've got unidentified traffic moving into your flight path. They don't answer our radio. Over."

O'Hara did not have to see Bimonte's violent shake of the head to know what the answer had to be. "Negative," he reported. "We're flying on fumes from the liquor locker now."

Ben watched the blips grow nearer. Horizontal separation was almost completely gone now. He could not be sure of vertical separation, but Ben sensed that the smaller plane was beneath the glide path of the jet.

Desperately he shouted, "O'Hara! Full flaps! Now!"

On the flight deck of 901, Michael O'Hara reacted without thinking. "Full flaps," he commanded.

Sam Allen's hand shot out and clenched around the flap levers. He shoved them all the way forward. Outside, there was a grinding sound as the huge metal flaps began to crawl back over the trailing edge of the swept wings. The jet's air speed dropped, and as the flaps took hold, increasing the lifting area of the wings, the great aircraft trembled against the extra resistance, and ballooned into the air an unexpected, precarious hundred feet.

Just ahead of the 707, the Piper Cherokee's occupants yelled with surprise and fear as a ponderous, light-blinking, space-filling black object swept over them and buffeted them with the force of its passing. The Cherokee was smashed brutally by the jet's wake and Jeff McGuire almost lost control. Jenny O'Hara was thrown against the side of the cockpit, striking her head, and when she could think again, she heard Jeff saying over and over, "Boy, that thing almost got us. It almost got us."

Numbly Jenny said, "That was Daddy's plane."

Inside the 707, passengers screamed as the plane seemed to strike a solid object. On the flight deck, fearing

92

the strain would be too much for metal to bear, O'Hara called, "Half flaps," and reduced his throttle settings another notch. His headphones crackled and Puzo's voice said, "Okay, you're past the bogey, Captain. But you're too high. Increase your rate of descent to seven hundred."

"Seven hundred," O'Hara repeated. "What happened to the other plane?"

"I don't know, sir," said the sergeant. "Their blip disappeared into the ground return. From the size of their signal, I'd say it was a light plane without radio." Grundig tapped his shoulder and pointed. "Wait a minute," said Puzo, "they're back on my scope. Half a mile behind you. They look all right."

"Thank God," said O'Hara.

In the First Class section, Jerry Weber stared out the window in sudden fright.

"What's happening?" he demanded. "I think someone's shooting at us." He fumbled under his seat for the small suitcase he had carried aboard.

Alarmed, Boo Brown said, "No they ain't, kid. We just hit an air pocket. Look, we're slowing down. We're landing."

Weber was not mollified. His hand continued the search for the suitcase. Desperately Boo Brown threw himself forward, forgetting that his seat belt was precariously fastened. It cut into his stomach and groin with a sharp pain that made him cry out. It was this sound rather than his movement that penetrated Weber's consciousness. "What is it?" asked the soldier. "What's the matter?"

Boo seized the opportunity. "Water," he gasped. "My . . . heart. I—Help me."

Jerry Weber jumped up and careened along the aisle, thrown from side to side by the erratic motion of the aircraft. "Stewardess!" he yelled. "Where are you? Why don't you listen? Where are you?"

Angela Shaw was nearest. She unstrapped herself and hurried to the young soldier. It's him, she thought. He's going to blow us all up. She thought of trying to hold his arm, but he looked terribly strong and violent, even though he was not a large man. He caught one of her wrists and jerked her toward Boo Brown's seat. "It's my friend," he said rapidly. "He's sick. He needs some water." Over Weber's shoulder, without the soldier being able to see what she observed, Angie saw Boo Brown shaking his head violently and beckoning her.

"The water's back there in the galley," she said. "You get it, I'll see if I can help him."

As Weber hurried to the galley, she got over to Brown as fast as the surge of the plane would permit her to move. While pantomiming the agony of a heart seizure, Boo whispered, "Sit down in the seat next to me. We've got to keep that bird from getting at his suitcase."

"What—" began Angie, and Boo cut her off with "Come on, baby, we both know this plane's being hijacked, and there's the joker who's doing it. He got all shook up a minute ago and now he's trying to get at his suitcase. We can't let him."

Quickly she stepped past him and sat in Weber's seat, blocking the access to the under-seat storage with her legs. When Weber returned, he found her holding Boo Brown's wrist, pretending to take his pulse.

"Here's the water," said Weber.

Gratefully Brown sipped it, spilling some down his shirt front.

"Maybe there's a doctor on board," Weber said, looking around wildly.

There was a gentle chime and the "No Smoking" sign went on.

"We're landing," said Angie. "I'd better stay with him. You take my seat up in the lounge. We'll get help as soon as we're on the ground."

Confused, the young soldier obeyed her instructions. He strapped himself in beside Hazel Martin. "My friend," he said numbly. "He's sick."

"I'm sorry," she said. "We'll be down soon."

"We better be," he said.

"Keep your air speed up!" shouted Ben Puzo. "You're sixty feet low. Get that nose up. Better, better . . . now you're on the path. Twenty seconds to touchdown. Don't try to be fancy, just let her fly right onto the ground. Fifteen seconds. You're doing fine, Captain. Kick in a hair of right rudder. Goddammit it, don't slip the bastard! Ten seconds. You're over the outer boundary, doing fine. Ease back on the stick a little, you're right on the beam, now let her down . . . down . . . DOWN!"

There was a long pause in the Operations Room.

His hands trembling, Ben Puzo leaned back and said, "I don't know exactly where in the hell you are, boys, but you're on the ground somewhere in the state of Washington."

"Thank God," whispered Angela Shaw.

In the forward lounge Hazel Martin lowered her head and began to sob.

Congressman Arne Lindner zipped up his fishing rod case and began to adjust his tie.

Elly Brewster began to talk wildly about vivid colors and sounds.

Lovejoy Welles locked herself in one of the aft rest rooms and threw up.

In Cleveland, Harvey Brandt received word from Seattle Control that 901 was on the ground. He bent his head and crossed himself.

Ben Puzo got up from his chair before the Controller console and strolled toward the door. "Men," he announced, "I have to go take a leak."

Herbert Kean burst into General Hotchkiss' office without knocking. "They're down!" he shouted. Hotchkiss looked up from his brandy glass and gave one of his rare smiles. "I know," he said. "Let's get drunk."

"You're on," said his secretary.

The President's private telephone rang. He picked it up himself. "Mr. President," said his secretary, "Flight 901 is on the ground in Seattle." The President sat silently for a moment, said, "Thank you," and hung up.

Orbiting Seattle, Allen Ross shouted at the pilot of the rented 707. "We missed them! We didn't get a shot." The pilot gave way to a burst of anger and said, "Too bad, you goddamned ghoul!" Surprised, Ross could only stare at him.

High over Lake Michigan, Paul Manchester responded to a gesture of the Vindicator's pilot and clamped a set of earphones onto his head. He heard the last part of a news flash: ". . . and despite zero visibility, the jet aircraft was safely landed at Seattle. More news as we get it from CBS Radio . . ."

Harriet Stevens, still strapped in her seat, arched her back as a new, not-to-be-ignored pain shot through her abdomen. My God, she thought, it's beginning. Her hand clenched around the arm rest and she breathed sharply through gritting teeth.

There was a squealing of tires as a light plane came out of the fog and skidded along the runway. Its pilot saw the big jet in front and, still leaning on his brakes, ground-looped off the paved runway into the soft mud alongside. The Piper Cherokee sheared off its landing gear and trembled to a stop, wing lights still blinking. Distantly the mournful wail of a crash truck sounded.

**THE EIGHTH HOUR**
(**The Second Half**)

A "Follow Me" truck appeared out of the fog and waited, lights blinking, in front of Flight 901. O'Hara flicked his landing beams, and the truck began to move slowly. Steered by its nose wheel, the 707 followed.

Inside, Jerry Weber unbuckled his seat belt and rushed back to the First Class section. Anxiously he looked down at Boo Brown.

"How you feeling, buddy?" he asked.

"Better," Boo said, deliberately stretching his legs out to block the entrance into the other seat where Angela Shaw sat, still holding his wrist. "Maybe it was just indigestion from this lousy airline food."

"How insulting . . ." Angie began, going along with the joke, anything to keep the young soldier from becoming agitated again. Her attempt failed.

"You listen to this man, you hear?" Weber said, glowering down at her. "Nobody listens, that's what's wrong with everything."

"Buddy," Boo said quickly, "you want to do me a favor?"

"Sure," said Weber. "Name it."

"I'm worried about my horn. I mean, man, that cello cost me a lot of bread. Would you get it out of the rack and hang onto it for me? I'm afraid that when these peasants start grabbing their coats and hats they might bruise Mama."

"Anything you say," Weber replied. "You helped me get on this plane. I won't forget that."

The soldier went forward to the coat rack and carefully removed the black case from its storage place. He started back toward Boo, who shook his head and waved toward the empty seat in the forward lounge. "Keep it out of the way of the thundering herd!" the black musician croaked. Weber hesitated, then nodded and took the instrument to the lounge seat and sat down.

"One more for the home team," Boo Brown murmured under his breath. By now the other three stewardesses were moving up and down the aisles. Hazel Martin stopped near Boo's seat.

"Angie?" she asked, puzzled, "Are you all right?"

"I've got to stay here," the girl said desperately. "We can't let—"

"Shut up!" Boo said harshly. To Hazel, "Move on, lady. We've got enough troubles. Don't attract any attention."

"Just a minute—" she began.

Angie cut her off. "Please, Hazel. I know what I'm doing. It's going to be all right."

The Head Stewardess hesitated, then moved away. Boo spoke in an undertone. "Don't look now, but our buddy is watching us like a hawk."

"What do you think he's got in the suitcase?" Angie asked.

"I don't know," said Boo Brown, "and I don't really want to find out. Let's just let the poor bastard step off the plane and get swallowed up by the FBI and have this thing over and done with."

At that moment a crash truck sped past them, going to the rear of the jet, lights blinking and siren wailing. The sound and sight of it caused Jerry Weber to stiffen. He looked around rapidly, fumbling at his seat belt.

"Oh, Jesus," mumbled Boo Brown, "I think I'm going to have a real heart attack if this crap keeps up." He looked around at Angie. "Sorry."

"I've heard worse," she said, trying to smile. "In fact, I'm thinking worse right now."

"Oh, oh," he said. "That truck did it. Here he comes."

Weber was on his feet, starting back toward them.

The loudspeaker crackled. "This is Captain O'Hara," it said. "Sorry about all the fog, but it couldn't be helped. Anyway, in case some of you were wondering about that crash truck that just passed, don't be alarmed. It isn't for us. It seems that a light plane which was following us in ran off the runway, and they're going out to give assistance. Let's hope no one was hurt. As for us, we'll be at the terminal building in a very few minutes, where we'll do our best to make up for the inconvenience you've suffered. As soon as the fog lifts, transportation will be provided down to San Francisco, or if you want to spend a while in Seattle as guests of Trans-America, why enjoy it. As you may know, the Space Needle and the Revolving Restaurant left over from the Seattle Fair are big attractions, very expensive, and if I were you I'd sock it to TA.

As for those of you who intended to continue on to Seattle on other flights out of San Francisco, don't worry. We won't charge you extra for the direct service. Now, if you look out the left side of the airplane, you'll see some fuzzy yellow lights through the Washington dew. That's the terminal building, where we'll be saying goodbye to you, and thank you for flying Trans-America. Better luck next time."

During O'Hara's announcement, Weber had relaxed and returned to his seat.

"We're almost there," Angie whispered.

"Yeah," groaned Boo Brown, "but look at that! Oh, Jesus, those stupid mothers!"

The girl peered through the fog. "All I see are the ground crew," she said.

"Ground crew!" spat the musician. "Since when do ground crew wear flak jackets under their raincoats! Oh, those idiots."

Angie felt a thrill of panic. "Maybe he won't notice," she said.

But the cluster of men grouped casually around the trucks and loading ramp had not escaped Jerry Weber's questing eyes. He leaned toward the window, looking from one group to another. There, in the cab of a TA truck, he clearly saw a sawed-off shotgun leaning against the seat back. And the protective body armor of several of the men showed clearly through the wet clinging of their outer garments.

"They're after me!" Weber shouted. Jane Burke, passing him with a tray of empty glasses, shrieked and dropped them. He pushed past her and started down the aisle toward Boo and Angie.

"Let's try to cool it," Boo began, but Angie had leaped

101

up and was shouting, "Help us! This man's a hijacker! Grab him!"

Shocked, unreacting, the men who might have intercepted Weber simply stared at the young soldier as he passed them. It was all too sudden, too unexpected. The moment froze in time for an instant, then was gone.

At Boo Brown's elbow, Weber said, "Let me in there!"

"No," said Boo, throwing himself toward the young soldier. But, once again, he forgot about his seat belt and it held him back just long enough for Weber to step away from his reach. At the same moment, Angie Shaw leaned forward and huddled between the seats, curled in a fetus ball blocking the opening under Weber's seat.

Now the other passengers began to react. Two men leaped up and began moving down the aisle toward the hijacker. One was Congressman Arne Lindner.

"No you don't!" yelled Weber. He scuttled backward into the lounge. Behind him, huddled in the galley where she had fallen, Jane Burke stood up and moved toward him, an empty wine bottle in her right hand. Weber was still fumbling in his jacket pocket when she closed her eyes and swung the bottle with all her might. She missed his head and Weber yelped with pain as the bottle struck his shoulder. He fell down in the aisle as the wine bottle clattered against the bulkhead.

"Get him!" shouted Boo Brown. He had his seat belt unfastened now and was forcing his mammoth bulk up by both hands on the seat rests. The interior of the cabin was filled with a confused din as some of the passengers began to scream, as others demanded to know what was going on.

Weber's hand came out of his jacket pocket, holding a black, pear-shaped object. A curved handle extended down its length. Weber squeezed the handle and thrust his index finger through a shining round ring.

"It's a grenade!" shouted the Congressman. "Get it away from him!" He threw himself toward the young soldier, but Weber rolled under the lounge table and as Boo Brown watched, horrified, plucked the ring from the grenade's top and threw the ring the length of the cabin.

"All right, you bastards!" Weber shrieked. "Come and get it. Just one of you touch me, come on, touch me and I'll let this lever go!"

The second man, a husky civilian wearing a plaid sports jacket, made a move toward him. Lindner caught his arm. "No," said the Congressman. "He's pulled the pin. If he releases that handle it goes off."

"That's right, Congressman!" yelled Weber. "You took your grenade training, huh? All right, get back to your seats. Every last one of you! Move!"

The men hesitated. "Better do like the man says," Boo Brown said quietly.

Jerry Weber stared at him. "I thought you were my friend," he complained. "You and me drank together. What kind of friend turns his buddy in?" He crawled out from under the table and leaned against it, trembling. The cello case rested against his feet. He kicked it aside. Boo winced. Near the galley, where she had thrown herself after trying to hit him with the bottle, Jane Burke began to sob. Weber whirled on her. "Shut up!" he bellowed. "In training they taught us not to trust the women. I should have remembered it. Shut your mouth. *Shut it!*"

Angie pushed past Boo and, keeping as much distance as possible between herself and the young soldier, knelt beside the frightened stewardess. "Shhh," she soothed.

103

"It's all right, Jane. Please be quiet."

"All right," Weber demanded of Boo, "hand me my suitcase. *Right now!*"

"Don't get shook, man," said Boo. "I'll get it." He did, and slid the suitcase over to the soldier. Weber unzipped it with one hand, still holding the grenade clutched in the other. "Why didn't you listen?" he said, struggling with the zipper. "All I wanted to do was make my shipment. But you had to spoil everything. Now what am I going to do?"

"Kid," Boo said gently, "you can still make your shipment. We're here, aren't we? The Captain will explain everything to your C.O. and—"

"What kind of a fool do you think I am?" demanded Weber. "No Stateside C.O.'s going to understand why I was justified to take necessary action to make that shipment. It takes a combat officer to understand what's necessary in an emergency. What do these Stateside Commandos know about emergency action?" Now the bag was open and as Boo watched, Weber took out a smoky-gray revolver and thrust it into his right trouser pocket. Brown glimpsed other metallic objects in the cloth suitcase before the young soldier slid it behind him on the lounge table. "You get back to your seat, buddy!" Weber commanded. "I'm not going to tell you again."

Reluctantly Boo returned to his seat and lowered himself into it.

Weber grabbed Angie's arm and pulled her to her feet. "Take me up to see the Captain!" he said. "Move!"

Jane Burke wailed again and covered her eyes with both hands. Angie stiffened herself with all the dignity she could muster and said, "I was just going to suggest

104

the same thing. I think the Captain would like to speak with you."

"We'll see about that, once I tell him where this plane's going next," Weber said. "I tried to be nice, I only wanted to come to Seattle, and look what's happened." He glared back at Boo Brown. "And it's all your fault!"

As he followed the young stewardess toward the flight deck, the big plane moved slowly closer to the loading ramp and the huddled groups of waiting men.

"I think we've had it," said TV commentator Allen Ross. "The pilot won't buzz the field for us. He says only a bat would go down in that soup. And that means when we get back to Boise, Mark Goddard is going to hoist our asses up on the flagpole for striking out."

"You can't shoot what you can't see," Happy Gunther said for the fifth time.

The other cameraman, a young ex-Signal Corps photographer named Preston Clemens hurried back. "Listen, Allen," he said, "there's something happening down there. The plane's on the ramp, but it stopped before it pulled up to the gate. Nobody's getting off. I just heard it on the radio."

Allen Ross cursed. "And here we are 14,000 feet overhead," he complained. "Goddard won't bother to fly us from the flagpole. He'll lock us up in the film library and let us starve. What does the pilot say?"

"No soap," Clemens replied. "As long as the weather's like this, he's not going down in it."

"Goddammit," shouted Ross, "that's what we hired him for!"

"Don't knock it," said Clemens. "Do you honestly want

to fly down into that mess? I'd rather be unemployed and alive."

Sourly Allen Ross said, "That's the trouble with you punk kids. No dedication."

"I was afraid of this," said General Hotchkiss, when the telephone call came. "You can't predict what an unbalanced person will do. I suppose I always really knew that Seattle was only the first lap."

"O'Hara reports the hijacker is a young GI," said Kean. "Apparently he's very disturbed about missing an overseas shipment. Maybe we could get his C.O. to speak with him by radio, promise him immunity or something."

"Herbert," the General said patiently, "that boy's guilty of air piracy. On the books the penalty is death. How are you going to give him immunity?"

"I didn't say give it to him, I just said promise."

"I'll forget you said that," Hotchkiss told his male secretary. "The word of an officer—and, for that matter, a gentleman—is sacred. How can you even suggest such a thing?"

"Because," said Kean, "I'm neither an officer nor a gentleman, and I'd tell that nut anything necessary to keep him from risking one life a single minute longer. And the second I got him disarmed, I'd hand him over to the FBI without a qualm. Furthermore, General, without wanting to be impertinent, I think you'd do the same thing, given the chance."

Hotchkiss sighed. "Yes," he said slowly, "I'm afraid I would."

After she unlocked the door to the flight deck, Angela Shaw said quickly, as the three airmen looked around,

106

"Captain, this gentleman wants to talk with you."

When he saw the grenade in the young soldier's hand, John Bimonte started to rise. "Sit down, Johnny," O'Hara said quietly. "All right, son, what's on your mind?"

"Get those guys out there away from the plane," said Weber.

"They're just ground crew," said the Captain.

"Get them away!" Weber repeated. "Nobody gets off this plane until they get away."

O'Hara shrugged. "Okay," he said. He pickped up the microphone and said, "Tower, this is 901. I have a request from one of the passengers that you move the ground crew back from this aircraft. Repeat, please move the ground crew back."

There was a brief pause, then, in his headphones, a voice said, "Captain O'Hara, is the passenger on the flight deck with you?"

"Affirmative," said O'Hara.

"Can he hear me?"

"Negative."

"I presume he's armed."

"That is an understatement," said O'Hara. "Listen, I suggest you carry out his suggestion first and let's discuss it later."

"We're trying to get an FBI agent into the emergency hatch directly under your flight deck," said the voice. "If you stall a little while, all you'll have to do is slide your seat away and we'll have an armed agent on board."

"That won't work," said O'Hara. "I'm asking, as commander of this aircraft, that you remove those men."

"We're concerned for the safety of your passengers," said the voice. "Trust us, Captain. We know what we're doing."

107

"I'm responsible for the safety of my passengers," O'Hara said, irritation rising in his voice, "and I repeat, get those men away from my aircraft."

"You're doing a great job, Captain," said the voice. "The bottom hatch is open. Just keep stalling and we'll have our man on board in a couple of minutes."

"Goddammit!" said O'Hara. "I said negative!"

"What's going on?" Weber asked nervously. He was perspiring heavily, O'Hara saw. If the boy's wet hand slipped on that grenade handle . . .

"I'm going to get rid of them," promised O'Hara. He switched frequencies. "Mayday!" he called. "Mayday!"

A new voice came into his headphones. "Mayday, we read you. This is Seattle Control. Who are you and what is your position?"

"I'm Trans-America Flight 901," said O'Hara, "and my position is right in front of your frigging terminal. Will you get those FBI men the hell away from this airplane before something unpleasant happens?"

The voice hesitated, then came back, "Captain, are you declaring an emergency? Since you're already on the ground, this is highly unusual—"

"You bet your ass I'm declaring an emergency, and it's caused by those cretins in their gray flannel suits. Get them out of here!"

The headphones were silent for a moment, then the voice said, "Captain, we have instructed the agents to move back."

"Good," said the pilot. "Keep them back." He removed the headphones and turned to the young soldier. "Okay," he said. "I got rid of them. Look out the window."

Weber did, and saw that the groups of men were dispersing.

"I still can't get off the plane," he said hesitantly. "They'll be out there waiting for me." He looked down at the grenade. "My hand's getting tired," he said quietly.

"Where's the pin?" O'Hara asked.

The soldier shook his head. "I don't know," he said. "I threw it away."

"How about I send the stewardess back there to look for it?" O'Hara asked.

"I don't need it," said Weber.

"You might," said the Captain. "Is that all right, son?"

"Oh, go ahead," Weber said. "But I won't need it. I don't care if I die. They're out to get me anyway. I might as well save them the trouble."

"Let's talk about that," said the Captain. "I've got a feeling things aren't as bad as you think they are. Angie, will you go back and look for the sergeant's pin?"

"I'm not a sergeant," said Weber. "I'm a Specialist Five."

Realizing that O'Hara was trying to tell her something, Angie asked, "What does it look like?"

"Oh, it's a little metal ring, isn't it—what does your father call you, soldier?"

"Jerome," said Weber. "But I like Jerry better."

"Do you mind if I call you Jerry?"

"I don't care," the soldier said dully, shifting the grenade in his sweating hand. Nearby, Bimonte winced. Weber looked at Angie. "What's the matter?" he asked. "Don't you listen? The Captain told you to find my pin. You never know. I might need it. But I don't think so."

Still searching, Angie said, "Where do you think it could be, Captain?"

"Oh, I don't know," O'Hara said casually. "You might check around the chutes. Anything could slide down them. Just about anything. Get right on it."

"You heard the Captain," said Weber. "Get right on it."

"Yes, sir," said Angela Shaw, leaving the flight deck.

"What's that out there?" said Weber, peering out the cockpit window.

"Where?"

"Under that truck? Look!" The boy's hand shook as he raised the grenade. "It's another one of them after me! I told you they wouldn't let me go!"

"Don't worry," said O'Hara. "I'll get rid of him. Is it okay if I open this window?" He nodded toward the pressure-sealed plexiglas to the left of his seat.

"Open it up but don't try anything," warned Jerry Weber. Then, at that moment, beneath the pilot's seat, he felt and sensed, rather than heard, a gentle tapping. He glanced at the crew members, who did not seem to notice anything.

"What's that?" Weber asked. "There's something underneath us."

"It must be the fuel truck plugging in," said O'Hara. "Let me get rid of that guy out there and then I'll take care of it." He got the window open and the damp fog penetrated into the cockpit. "Hey, you!" O'Hara called, "Get away from here."

The man crouched under the truck stared at him. "What?" he asked, incredulously.

"You heard what I said," O'Hara shouted. "As commander of this aircraft, I'm ordering you away from us."

"Buster," said the man, "I'll go when I'm damned good and ready. We're only trying to help you."

"Mister," O'Hara said grimly, "there's a man right behind me with a pistol and a hand grenade with the pin out. I don't think he'll let go of the grenade, but if you

110

don't start moving before I count to three, I'm going to borrow his pistol and shoot you myself!"

The distant man stared at him. "You're nuts too!" he shouted.

"One," said O'Hara. "Two."

The man faded into the fog.

"Hey!" said Weber, laughing, "You really put it to him. Would you really have borrowed my pistol to shoot him?"

"In one second more," O'Hara said grimly. And, surprised at himself, he knew that he would have.

Now he pounded his foot on the metal deck. "Listen, down there!" he bellowed. "Get the hell out! We hear you."

"I think we might want some fuel," said the soldier. "Let him go ahead and put it in."

"He's loading the wrong tank," said O'Hara. He stamped his foot again. "Get going!" he shouted. He looked at the boy sharply. "We're almost empty," he said. "I don't think we could go fifty miles."

"Well, tell them to fill it up," said Jerry Weber. "I just got an idea. You know, Captain, you're a good man. I think we'll get along together just fine. You can call me Jerry."

"All right, Jerry," said O'Hara, reaching for the microphone. "But if they bring the fuel truck up they'll need a couple of men too."

"That's all right," said Weber. "I know you won't let them play any tricks on me. And once we're all fueled up again, we'll be on our way and everything will be all right. Because watching you take command there, I just figured out how to make everything good again. It takes a real commander to understand what an emergency is,

111

do you get what I mean?"

"I'm not sure," said O'Hara. "Where do you want us to go next?"

The boy's eyes were too bright and his voice was too high, but he had stopped sweating. He leaned back against one of the VHF radios and said, as if it were a great discovery, "Okinawa."

**THE NINTH HOUR**
(The First Half)

O'Hara's reference to "chutes" had not been lost on Angela Shaw. The Captain hoped that the young soldier on the flight deck beside him would think he was referring to parachutes, although such safety devices are not normally carried aboard commercial aircraft. So far as O'Hara knew, the only parachute aboard any jet liner was the one rumored to be stored on Air Force One for the extremely unlikely possibility that the President of the United States might be able to use it in the event of midair breakup. Other than that, parachutes were regarded as useless weight.

The chutes he meant, and the ones that the four stewardesses, with the help of several male passengers, were now quietly lowering to the cement beneath the plane, were the emergency evacuation chutes, long, rubberized canvas slides designed to help survivors get out of a

113

downed plane fast. Today's utilization was unusual, but effective. One chute was already in position below the forward galley, and uneasy passengers were lining up, shoes in hands, observing the stewardesses' admonitions "not to make a sound." Two men had lowered themselves to the ground by hanging from the lip of the emergency hatch and dropping twelve feet to the damp hardtop, and were now holding the chute taut.

"Okay," whispered Angie to the first passenger, a stocky woman who clutched a fur coat possessively as if it were going to be taken away from her. "Don't worry about a thing, it's just like Coney Island. When you get on the ground, don't go toward the front of the plane. Don't let anyone in the cockpit see you. Go back toward the tail, and wait. We'll send someone to take you into the terminal. Do you understand?"

The woman bobbed her head. She tried to say something, but it came out as a choked, throat-clearing sound. She sat on the edge of the hatch, clutched her coat closer to her bossom, and then slid into the fog like a battleship down the ways.

"Next," hissed Angie. A man crowded toward her. "Wait your turn," she told him angrily. "There's a line—"

"I'm not going anywhere," said the man. She saw that it was Congressman Lindner. "Listen, we've got some trouble back here. Can you come?"

Angie looked at Lovejoy Welles, who was helping her. "I can handle it here," the trainee said, her voice not quite steady.

As Angie followed the Congressman back to the Tourist Section, Lindner asked, "Is there a doctor on board?"

"None were listed on the manifest," she answered, pushing past the line of people crowding the aisle. "It's

114

the first thing we check."

"I'm afraid we're going to need one," he said. "How many passengers boarded in New York?"

"Ninety," she replied, puzzled.

He smiled tightly. "Well, it looks as if ninety-one are going to get off."

O'Hara had ordered the refueling, and it was in progress. He warned Operations to keep law enforcement officers away from the aircraft, and so far as he could tell, they were obeying his order. There had been one final thumping sound from the compartment beneath his seat, perhaps the outer hatch being slammed shut, and now the three airmen and the hijacker sat quietly in the green and red gloom of the flight deck. O'Hara wanted to keep the young soldier talking, keep him interested, and above all keep him from returning to the passenger cabin. He hoped fervently that Angela had caught his meaning about the emergency chute exists.

"Listen, son," he said, "this plane can't make it to Okinawa. Do you know how far that is?"

Weber grinned. "Don't try to kid me, Captain," he said. "Sure, I know how far Okinawa is. It's around six thousand miles by the great circle route."

"Just about," O'Hara agreed. "This plane can't fly that distance."

"Don't kid me," Weber repeated, smiling as if this were a pleasant game.

"I'm not."

"This is a Boeing 707 dash 320. It's got a range of more than seven thousand miles. I saw it in that booklet from the seat pocket."

"This is a 220," O'Hara said, feeling sweat break out on

his forehead. He hoped the soldier had no way of knowing that the 320's had been reassigned to continental United States runs after the 747 jumbo jets began flying the over-water routes. "The 320 is the Intercontinental model. But the aircraft we're on is just for Stateside runs."

"It's all too complicated for me," Weber said conversationally. "I trust you to get us there, Captain. You're a man who knows his job. You'll figure out a way."

"Why Okinawa?" asked Sam Allen. O'Hara glared at him.

"Who's that?" demanded Weber.

"My First Officer," O'Hara said. "What you'd call a co-pilot."

"Okay," Weber said. "What's the matter, co-pilot, don't you ever listen? Didn't you hear me tell the Captain here that it would take a combat officer to know what was necessary in an emergency? You don't think I'm going to find any combat officer in Seattle, do you? But you get me to Okinawa, let me report in early, not late, and tell the C.O. what I had to do to get there, and he'll understand. The Captain here understands, because he's a good commander."

"I don't know, Jerry," O'Hara said cautiously. "You might be better off here in Seattle. After all, you're not that late."

Weber shook his head violently. "Uh-UH!" he said. "I mean, I'm not just late, I had to commandeer the use of this airplane. A combat man would understand that. But not one of these Statesides Commandos." He leaned forward. "Captain, I trust you. Don't tell me things won't work out for me in Okinawa. If I believed that was the truth, I might just as well let go of this handle and forget the whole thing."

116

"I was just presenting all sides of the argument," O'Hara said quickly. "If you don't mind the extra flight time, I guess it's okay with us."

Weber grinned. "I knew that's what you'd say," he said. "Boy, you can sure tell the real ones from the PX Infantry, you know what I mean?" His hand shifted on the grenade, almost dropped it. "Man"—he laughed—"I just about pulled a boo-boo there. Hey, where is that girl with my pin? I'd just as soon lock this baby on safe, if that's all right with you. We don't want any accidents, do we?" He looked around. "Maybe I'd better go back and help her."

"No," O'Hara said, "let my co-pilot do that. I want you to sit up here with me and help plan our route. I need all the help I can get. Sam, will you go back and give Angie a hand? That pin may have slid down inside one of the chutes, and I want everything out of them in the next five minutes. We're just about through refueling."

"Sure, Mike," said Allen.

"Call him Captain," Weber said sharply. "You're nothing but a lousy co-pilot. What do you know?"

"Not much," Sam Allen answered bitterly. O'Hara shot a warning glance at him. "Okay," said the First Officer. "I'll see if I can find your pin, soldier."

"You do that," Weber said as the flier passed him in the narrow corridor. He waited until Sam had gone through the door and then laughed. "Did you see his face?" he choked. "He wanted to grab this grenade so bad he could taste it. Where do you get your co-pilots, Captain?"

"He's young," said O'Hara. "Listen, Jerry, if we're going to fly together, you might as well call me Mike. We're not too formal up here where the work gets done."

"I know what you mean," said Weber. "The good ones don't have to wave their bars around. They get the respect because they earn it. But I think I'd better call you Captain, for now, anyway. I mean, you don't know yet if I'll come through, do you? It has to work both ways."

"Okay," said O'Hara. "Leave it there for now. But any time you want to call me Mike, you just go ahead and do it. Listen, Jerry, why don't you sit up here in the right seat? You can see better, and you and I have to go over the course and stuff like that."

Dubiously Jerry Weber said, "Is it all right? I never flew a plane before."

"We let the autopilot do most of the work," O'Hara said. "Come on."

Carefully the young soldier slid into the padded seat. He looked out over the curved nose of the jet. "Wow," he said. "It sure looks different from up here. I mean, back there it's like riding in a Greyhound bus. But here's where the action is. What are all these dials and stuff?"

"They tell you how fast the aircraft is going, how high it is, and so on," said O'Hara, still playing for time. "This one shows me what our flight attitude is. It's called the artificial horizon. See that little airplane inside? If it's up above that horizontal line, I know I'm climbing. If it's below, I know I'm losing altitude. And if one wing comes up, I can see that I'm in a turn."

"How about that?" said Weber. "It's real easy. I bet I could fly one of these things with just a little work."

"You might be able to at that," said O'Hara. "Let me check you out on this instrument panel. It's simpler than it looks. See this one that looks like a clock? It shows how high you are."

"Why does it say we're a hundred feet up?" demanded the soldier. "We're on the ground, aren't we?" He looked out the window into the fog.

O'Hara laughed easily. "Sure we are," he said. "But we set that one for sea level, and this field is built on a hill. We're about a hundred feet above the Sound, that's why it's reading high."

Jerry Weber stared at the altimeter. "I hear what you're saying," he said, "but what good does it do you to know how high you are above sea level if you're flying through a bunch of mountains, four, five thousand feet up in the air?"

"Son," said the pilot, "I think you've got the makings of a genuine airman. That's the first question they teach you to ask in flight school. Here, I'll show you how it works. First, you've got to remember there are two altitudes to keep in mind: true height, and height over terrain . . ."

"Captain," Weber said softly.

"Yeah?"

"There never was any bomb. I made it all up. I'm sorry for lying to you."

O'Hara looked down at his hands pressed against the control yoke. They were trembling.

"That's all right, son," he said.


"How's it going?" Sam Allen asked Lovejoy Welles.

"We've got two chutes working," the trainee said. "Five or six more passengers to go up here, and a dozen or so in the rear and they'll all be out. Jane's down below, guiding them to the terminal."

As she spoke, two more men slid down the chute, holding their shoes to keep from puncturing the rubberized fabric.

"Where's Angie?"

"Some man came up and got her a couple of minutes ago," she said. "She's back in Tourist."

"Did anyone find that damned grenade pin?"

The trainee looked bewildered. "What pin?" she asked. "We haven't even been looking for one."

Sam shook his head and began casting his eyes around the cabin. He saw a dull glint in one corner, near the magazine rack. Bending over, he picked up what looked like a cotter key with a round wire hoop projecting from one end. "This must be it," he said. He put it in his pocket. "I'll go back and see what's with Angie."

Angela was administering oxygen to Harriet Stevens, who was only half-conscious. Near her stood Congressman Arne Lindner. "What's the matter?" asked Sam Allen.

"I think she's going into labor," Angie said. "She fainted a while ago, but maybe that was because she's so frightened. Sam, I checked the list and there's no doctor aboard. Can we get one out here from the terminal."

Allen looked back toward the flight deck. "I don't know," he said. "No telling what that might do to our friend up there. Do you think she's that bad?"

"Millions of babies get born every year," said the girl. "But she's bad enough that I can promise you she's not sliding down any emergency chute. We're going to have to carry her off."

Allen sighed. "I'll do what I can," he said. "Let's get everybody else out first, though. Once that dingaling comes back and sees these empty seats, all hell is going to break loose."

He started back to the flight deck. The First Class section had been cleared now, except for one man who sat quietly in a forward seat. It was Boo Brown, the huge black musician.

"Can I help you?" Allen asked.

Boo shook his head wryly. "No chance," he said. "I

120

tried. I just can't bring myself to slide down that thing. I'm afraid I'd go right through it. Man, when I fall down on my back, somebody has to come along and roll me over before I can get up again. I go out the front door or not at all."

The First Officer studied the musician's girth. "I guess you're right," he said finally. "Well, don't worry. We won't bail out and leave you."

Boo Brown gave a little wave of his hand as Allen went forward. Lovejoy Welles was standing by the open emergency hatch.

"Go on," Allen said. "Get the hell out of here."

"I was going to," the trainee said. "But there's someone coming up the chute."

"Up?" Disbelievingly Allen looked out into the gloom. He saw a slim girl pulling herself up the emergency chute, eyes squinting with effort. Her hair was mussed and there was a clot of blood over her right ear.

A few feet below the lip of the hatch, she thrust one hand toward him and gasped, "Help me up!" He caught her wrist and lifted her into the airplane. She fell against the bulkhead, coughing. "Thanks," she choked. "Where's my daddy?"

Numbly Allen said, "Everyone's off but the crew. Why did you come back?"

"Come back?" the girl replied. "I just got here. And my daddy *is* the crew. He's the pilot."

Allen looked at her closer. He had seen this face in dozens of photographs. "My God," he said. "Jenny O'Hara!"

"Are they through fueling?" asked Jerry Weber.

"Almost," said O'Hara. "Now, this dial shows hydraulic pressure. You need that for your brakes and—"

"I'm tired, Captain," said the young soldier. "Listen, where's that co-pilot of yours with my pin? This thing's getting heavy. I almost dropped it a minute ago."

Before O'Hara could answer, the door opened and Sam Allen returned, a strange expression on his face.

"Here," said the First Officer, holding out the bit of twisted metal to Weber. "I found your pin."

"Thanks," said the soldier, taking it.

"Was it in the chutes?" asked the Captain.

"Yeah," said Allen. "But don't worry. They're empty now. Except—"

Carefully Jerry Weber fitted the ring back into the neck of the grenade. "Got it!" he said. He tossed it casually to O'Hara. "Catch!"

O'Hara juggled it. Weber watched him carefully. The Captain weighed the grenade in one hand. "Heavy," he said. "I didn't know they were so heavy."

"What are you going to do with it?" Weber asked softly.

"Give it back," said O'Hara, tossing it to the soldier. "I sure in hell don't want it."

Weber laughed. "You're a good man, Charlie Brown!" he said. "I just wanted to see what you'd do. Listen, I don't think I'm going to learn to fly this plane today. Why don't we take off and head for Okinawa?"

"Would you mind if I put the passengers off first?" asked O'Hara.

"Why? Do they have something against the Far East? Or is it my company?"

"It's just that each passenger on board eats up five minutes of fuel," said O'Hara. "If we take off with only five of us on board, we'll have another thousand miles of range, and what's more, we'll get there sooner, too."

"That makes sense," Weber said. "Well, why not? I

don't see why I should give a bunch of civilians a free trip overseas. Okay, it's all right with me."

"Sam," the Captain began, "go back and tell the passengers—"

That was as far as he got. The door was flung open and Jenny O'Hara burst in. "Daddy," she sobbed, "there's some woman back there screaming and moaning and they wouldn't let me in to see you—"

Behind her was Angie Shaw, white-faced. "I tried to stop her, sir," she told O'Hara, "but—"

"*Quiet!*" yelled Jerry Weber. "Who's that? What woman's screaming and hollering? I'm not going to hurt anyone—"

"Close the door," O'Hara said quickly.

Angie started to push it onto the latch, but Weber stepped forward. "Wait just one damned minute," he said. "What's going on out there?" He pushed his way over to Jenny. "Who are you?" he asked.

"That's my daughter, Jenny," O'Hara said. "Jenny, go to your seat. I'll be back in a few minutes—"

"You never said you had a daughter on this flight," Weber said. His eyes flicked from one crewman to another. "Somebody's playing tricks on me. Come on, Captain! Maybe I've been giving you credit for being a better man than you are. Let's go back and see what that woman is hollering about."

"Don't you yell at my daddy!" Jenny told him grimly.

The soldier laughed. "A chip off the old block," he commented. "Are you coming, Mr. Pilot? Or do I take this pin out again?"

"Lead the way," said O'Hara.

"What was it like?" demanded a reporter, thrusting his microphone into the face of a woman who appeared out

123

of the fog, carrying her shoes in one hand. She burst into sobs and brushed past him. The reporter followed her. "Did he threaten anyone? Does he have a gun? What does he look like?"

"Leave me alone," choked the woman.

"Hey," said a second reporter, "the caterer's van is going out."

"Come on!" yelled the first. "Let's hitch a ride!"

"O'Hara's in real trouble," said the Seattle Operations Officer. The Captain of Flight 901 had left his flight deck microphone open, so the ground personnel could hear everything that went on on the flight deck. "No telling what that guy's going to do when he sees the passengers are gone."

His assistant said, "The caterer's truck is on its way out there. We'd better recall it."

"They don't have a radio," said the Operations Officer. "Send a jeep, see if you can head them off."

"You lied to me!" shouted Jerry Weber.

"I asked you if we could let the passengers off," O'Hara said calmly.

"You put them off first and then you asked me," the young soldier shot back. "I thought I could trust you. You didn't listen to me at all. You kept me up there with all that talk about how to fly this plane and while I was trusting you, you were going around my back and letting people get off before I said they could."

"What does it matter?" asked the Captain. "We're still here. And we'll take you to Okinawa, just like you want. Look, Jerry—"

"Don't you call me Jerry!" the soldier grated, slashing

out with his right hand. It caught O'Hara against the bridge of the nose and the pilot fell back against the lounge table, stars blazing inside his head. Sam Allen made a growling noise deep in his throat and started toward Weber.

"You just come ahead!" Weber said softly, pointing his revolver at the First Officer.

"Hold it, Sam!" O'Hara ordered. Then, to Weber: "Okay, son. You're right. I did trick you. But I did it to protect my passengers. You can understand that. You know it's a commander's first duty to look out after his men. I wasn't sure you'd let them off and we both know the flight to Okinawa is going to be dangerous. So I assumed the responsibility. I know now that I should have consulted with you first."

Weber's attitude loosened slightly. "I don't know what to make of it all," he admitted. "All right, Captain. I'll give you the benefit of the doubt. But no more tricks. I want you to listen to me from now on."

"I will," O'Hara promised.

They heard a sobbing moan from the rear cabin.

"What's that?" Weber demanded.

Defiantly Angie Shaw said, "We've got a woman back there ready to have a baby. You've got to let us take her off."

Weber stared at her. "Take her off?" he repeated. "What kind of bastard do you think I am? Sure you can take her off. Hell, I'm not that bad."

Flustered, Angie said, "Oh. Well, thank you. Captain, can I put down the emergency ramp?"

"Go ahead," O'Hara said.

But at that moment the caterer's van arrived. It made a circle around the plane and began to back up toward the plane. Inside its open doors, two reporters crouched, and their cameras, pointed at the 707, looked like black, huge weapons.

"FBI!" Weber yelled. He lifted his revolver and began shooting.

**THE NINTH HOUR**
(**The Second Half**)

The bullets spanged off the concrete, throwing up white dust and whining as they spun into the fog.

"Hold it!" shouted O'Hara. "That's just the caterer's truck."

Weber whirled on him. "Get rid of them!"

"They're only photographers," O'Hara persisted.

The young soldier jammed his pistol barrel into the Captain's ribs. "Make them go away."

O'Hara brushed away from the weapon and went over to the edge of the open hatch. He did not have to shout at the driver of the truck. It was already disappearing into the fog at top speed.

"What's going on here?" demanded Weber. "Everybody's playing games. Captain, get this airplane moving."

"We can't!" gasped Angie. "That woman—"

"Captain . . ." the soldier said softly, clicking back the

127

hammer of his revolver and pointing it directly at the stewardess' head.

"We can't take off with those chutes dragging," O'Hara said.

Weber's voice, when it came, was ragged and taut. "Drag them until we're on the runway," he grated. "Move!"

O'Hara picked up the intercom microphone. "Allen, this is O'Hara. Inform the Tower we're proceeding to the end of the runway for takeoff."

There was a long pause. "Yes, sir," said Allen's voice.

"Please," whispered Angela Shaw. "Let us put that woman off. It'll only take a minute."

"No."

"She might die."

"We might all die," said Weber. "You brought this on yourselves. I wanted to be nice, but you wouldn't listen to me. All right. Now watch what happens when you don't listen."

There came a sound from the corner of the cabin. It was a surpressed, frightened gasp.

Forgotten in the excitement, Lovejoy Welles was still aboard. Weber glared at her. "They told us not to trust the women," he said. "Do you know what the women over there do? They carry grenades down their dresses and when you're not looking, *blam!*" He whirled on O'Hara. "Why isn't this plane moving?"

"My guess is we're waiting for a Follow Me jeep to lead us out to the end of the runway," said the Captain. "We'd never find it ourselves in this fog."

"Well tell them to get a move on!" ordered the soldier. O'Hara started toward the flight deck. "And listen," the soldier went on, "don't get any funny ideas up there

128

about locking the door and playing tricks on me. I've still got these women back here."

"There won't be any tricks," O'Hara promised. He opened the door and stepped inside.

"Mike," said John Bimonte, white-faced, "we're not going to take off again, are we? This crate can't make it to Okinawa."

"We may have to," O'Hara said. "We'll plot our first leg to Dutch Harbor, then up the Aleutian Chain, skirt the Kurile Islands and make landfall on Hokkaido. We can refuel at Sapporo or Tokyo if we have to."

"But the kid's nuts," Bimonte persisted. "He might just decide to tell us to steer this bus to the moon."

"He might," O'Hara agreed, "but meanwhile he's back there with a pistol pointed at Angie's head. What do you suggest I do?"

"Mike," said Sam Allen, "I've got Operations for you."

O'Hara slipped into the headphones, picked up the microphone. "This is O'Hara," he said. "We have been ordered to make an immediate takeoff, destination Okinawa. Will you instruct the ground crew to lead us out to the end of the operating runway?"

"Very well, Captain," said a voice. "I have the District Director of the FBI here. He wants to speak with you."

"Put him on."

"Captain?" said a new voice. "The Gate Officer tells me two stewardesses and four passengers did not deplane."

"That's correct," said O'Hara. "Not to mention three of us up here on the flight deck. One of the passengers is the hijacker, one is a pregnant woman about to give birth, one is a man too fat to go down the emergency chute and the last is a Congressman giving assistance to the sick woman."

"I have received orders from the White House, sir," said the voice, "to get Congressman Lindner off that plane safely at all costs."

"It might cost more than you think," O'Hara said. "This boy is dangerous. He's heavily armed. I'd suggest you let me handle the situation."

"Captain," said the FBI man, "I don't blame you for being frightened. But men like Weber are our business. I assure you, when he sees capture is inevitable, he'll surrender without further incident. He's not a hardened criminal."

"What do you intend to do?" asked O'Hara, moving the throttles forward. The huge jet began to creep slowly along the concrete.

"I have two snipers stationed at the end of the runway," said the voice. "If the hijacker persists in forcing you to take off again, they'll shoot out the tires. We had good luck with that during one other hijack attempt. The man was taken without injury to himself or others."

"Listen to me, mister," O'Hara said, "and listen good. I'm in command of this aircraft, and nobody's shooting out tires, windows, or anything else. Do you read me?"

"I'm afraid, sir," said the voice, "that I am not under your command. We will have to handle the situation as we think best."

O'Hara cursed and slammed the microphone into its cradle. "John," he told the Flight Engineer, "I want you to go back and start cutting those emergency chutes away. We probably aren't going to have time to do it when we get down to the end of the runway. I'll warn the kid you're coming."

He picked up the intercom microphone. "Jerry," he said, "this is Mike O'Hara. I'm sending John Bimonte, our

Flight Engineer, back to cut away those emergency chutes so we can close the hatches. We can't take off unless they're secured. Also, would Congressman Lindner please come up to the flight deck? Jerry, it's all right. The FBI is giving me a hard time and I want the Congressman to pull some rank on them. Is that okay with you? Angie, show Jerry how to use the intercom."

He waited, and then Weber's voice blasted into his ears. "Okay, Captain," said the young soldier. "But remember, no tricks."

Lindner entered and O'Hara explained the situation to him. The Congressman's lips tightened. "Those stupid bastards," he said.

"Just talk into this," O'Hara said, handing him the microphone.

"This is Congressman Lindner," the FBI man heard over the loudspeaker in the communications room. "Who am I talking with?"

"Whidden, District Director," said the FBI man.

"Okay, Whidden, you listen to me and you listen good. I forbid you to take any action to detain this aircraft without the express permission of Captain O'Hara. Do you understand me?"

"Yes, sir," said Whidden, flustered, "but it's my duty to protect lives and property—"

"Protect them then!" flared the Congressman. "Don't come around endangering us all with your stupid cops and robbers act. Whidden, I'm repeating, I forbid you to risk damage to this aircraft and those aboard it. Is anyone there from the CAB?"

"FAA, sir," said the Operations Officer. "CAB doesn't get into actual operations. How can I help you?"

"See that Whidden keeps his snipers away from us."

The Operations Officer hesitated. "I'm afraid," he said

slowly, "that I have no authority over the FBI."

"Well," Lindner said grimly, "I know who does. Have you been taping this?"

"Yes, sir."

"Good. Call this number—" And then Lindner recited the highly classified private number of the President of the United States. "Ask for the President, tell him I instructed you to do so, and then play back this tape from when I asked Mr. Whidden his name. Do it right now."

"Yes, sir," said the Operations Officer.

"Just a minute," said Whidden. "That won't be necessary, Mr. Congressman. I'll instruct my men to hold their fire."

"Good."

"You understand, sir," the FBI man went on, "that I am only trying to do my job."

"I understand," said the Congressman. "Now suppose we both let Captain O'Hara do his."

The Vindicator's pilot tapped his headphones and Paul Manchester adjusted his own.

"Flight 901 is moving again," he heard. "Although most of the passengers and two of the stewardesses slid to safety on emergency exit ramps, five crew members and four passengers still remain aboard. The aircraft has been refueled, and reports from our correspondent on the scene state that the hijacker has now ordered the pilot to fly to the island of Okinawa."

Paul pressed his throat microphone. "Did they name the stewardesses who got off?" he asked the pilot.

"Sorry, I didn't hear any names," was the answer. "Listen, Mr. Manchester, this is a pretty good airplane, but I don't think we can make Okinawa with it. I'd better set down at McCord Air Force Base. Sorry things didn't work out better."

"Maybe she got off," Paul said.

But then the radio voice returned and began listing the passengers and crew still aboard Flight 901, and he heard clearly, through the static, "Stewardess Angela Shaw of New York City . . ."

"Listen, they're taking off again!" TV Commentator Allen Ross yelled at the pilot of the rented 707. "They're going to Okinawa. Can we follow them?"

"You've got to be kidding," said the pilot.

"What do you think we hired you for?" Ross demanded. "Give me a yes or no!"

"Well," the pilot said thoughtfully, "he'll probably be taking the route up past Dutch Harbor, out along the Chain. Yeah, we can follow part of the way. But we don't have enough fuel to make the Japanese mainland. I can let you have him as far as Adak, but we'll have to put down for fuel there. By the time we get airborne again, we'll be an hour behind."

"Adak's better than nothing!" Allen said happily. "What do we do now? Wait for him on top of these clouds?"

"If he's really going to Okinawa, we ought to be able to pick him up just off Vancouver Island. The fog doesn't go out to sea more than a couple of miles. It'll be clear from there on."

"Great, great! Let's get going." Ross hurried back to the cabin and told Happy Gunther, "Guess what? We're going to Adak."

"Where's Adak?" asked the cameraman.

"Ah, I knew it," Brigadier General (Retired) Marion Hotchkiss said slowly. "It wasn't in the cards for us to get off that easily. Herbert, do you think I'd better bypass a few channels and talk to O'Hara myself?"

"I wouldn't," said his secretary. "From all reports, he's handling things as well as any man could. If you get into the act, it might cause him to tighten up."

"I wish I were at those controls," said the General. "It's always easier to be under the gun yourself then to send others to do it."

"How about some more brandy, General?"

"I don't think so," said Hotchkiss. "All right. Alert our personnel all the way up to Fairbanks. Contact Shepherd at Pan Am and tell him what's happening. He'll give us facilities along the Chain and in Japan, if we need them. Make sure those passengers in Seattle get every assistance. And tell our man out there not to go shoving releases at them. If they sue, they sue. I don't want them annoyed today."

"Right, sir," said Kean.

"As for the crew still on board. Set up a series of calls to their wives. I want to talk to the stewardesses' parents. I don't know how much I can help, but if I don't do something, I'll go mad."

"I'll get right on it, sir."

Hotchkiss sat quietly, looking up at the ten-foot map of the United States, crisscrossed with red strips indicating TA routes. Where once they had seemed to him proud banners of achievement, now the markers were only reminders that any moment, any day, the latent insanity that seems to possess the world more and more can break out wantonly, destructively, without warning . . .

Dazed, pain thrusting angry fingers through her body, Harriet Stevens looked fearfully around the empty cabin.

Angela Shaw was bent over her. She had pulled out the two arm rests to turn the three Tourist Class seats into a rude couch.

"We're moving?" Harriet asked.

"Shhh," Angie whispered.

"I hate to be so much trouble," Harriet said. "My mother warned me that something might happen. But I was supposed to have at least two more weeks yet."

"Don't worry," Angie said. "You're no trouble. Just relax and try to be comfortable."

"Where is everyone?"

Angela started to answer, but then there were chopping noises from the rear of the cabin and a male voice called, "Angie! Give me a hand, will you? I can't get this chute clear."

"You just lie quiet," Angie said. "I'll be right back. Try not to worry."

The stewardess went away, and Harriet Stevens lay on her side, staring at the seat backs just a foot away from her face. She saw papers protruding from the sewn-in pocket . . . a map, a *Trans-America Magazine,* and a heavy brown paper bag with little plastic tabs at its top. "For Motion Sickness." What about morning sickness? She turned her head. What was wrong? Why was she alone in this huge airplane? What was going on in the rear, where she could hear strange noises? Why was the plane still moving, with nobody aboard but her? She started to call the stewardess, but another spasm of pain tore through her body, and instead she threw back her head and screamed.

"There's the runway," Sam Allen said. "We'd better get Johnny up here for the takeoff."

"We can't take off until he's secured those hatches," O'Hara said. The two men were alone now on the flight deck. The Congressman had just returned to the passenger compartment, after O'Hara had told him, "Listen, there's a hatch down here under my seat. You can go through it and get out when I stop at the end of the runway for clearance."

"I think I'd better stay," said Lindner. "I helped the boy get on this plane. I feel responsible for him."

"We're all responsible," said O'Hara. "I'd feel better if you got off."

"I'd feel better if I stayed," said the Congressman.

O'Hara shrugged. "Suit yourself," he said.

The door opened. It was John Bimonte. "The emergency hatches are secure," he reported.

"Where's our number one passenger?"

"He's sitting back there talking with that fat guy."

"Okay," said O'Hara. "Takeoff check list."

As the litany of procedure, of routine, of actions that had been repeated a thousand times, of unspoken prayer began, two FBI men waited in the fog with high-powered rifles. One started to lift his weapon, then lowered it slowly.

"Why didn't you get off with the rest of them?" Weber asked the musician.

Boo Brown smiled. "Man, I tried," he said. "I just had too much lard to go down that rubber sliding board."

"I'm glad you stayed," said Weber. "You and me are buddies. You'll like Okinawa." He reached down below the table. "Look. Here's your cello. I'm sorry I dropped it before. I was excited."

"No harm done," Boo said. "Why don't you strap it in

136

that seat over there?"

"Don't you want it here beside you?"

"Where would you sit then?"

To Boo's surprise, tears began to roll down Jerry Weber's thin cheeks. "I said it before," the young soldier whispered. "You're my buddy. You *listen* to me. You understand that I'm not bad."

"Why don't we have a drink?" Boo suggested, reaching for his flask. "I could use one."

"Let me put your instrument over there first," said Weber. He placed the cello case in a First Class seat and strapped it in carefully, gently. When he came back his eyes were dry, but shining.

"Have a little juice," Boo said, handing him a small plastic cup. "I guess the stews are busy, but I carry these little goodies just in case. Like it says on my jug, BE PREPARED."

"You know," Weber said, sipping, "I'd sure like hear you play sometime. Do you think I will?"

"You just know you will," said Boo.

"What kind of musician are you?"

Boo smiled. "Well," he said slowly, "there's them that says I'm pretty good, and there's them that says I'm rotten."

"Who says you're rotten?" demanded the young soldier. "You tell me and I'll fix them for you."

"Many thanks, son," said the musician. "I don't take it too much to mind. You see, the cello is supposed to be a classical instrument. But me, I play jazz on it. Worse than that, I play *le jazz hot,* if you know what I mean."

"I'm not sure," said Weber.

"Well," said Boo Brown, "it's like I took Dizzy Gillespie and Peggy Lee and George Lewis and rolled them all up

137

in that big old Mama, you know what I mean? Dig? It comes out a sound nobody ever heard before. Half the time I don't even use a bow. I mean, I *pluck* Mama, and she sings like a nightingale on a cherry branch."

There came a low, long moaning from the other cabin. Boo's face darkened. "Hey, buddy," he said softly, "can't you see your way clear to let that poor woman out of here before we take off? I mean, she's real sick."

"I know she is," Weber said frantically. "Listen, don't try to make me upset. I'm upset enough already. I wanted to let her off. But they tried to play tricks on me. I know why they want to let that ramp down. They want those FBI men with their tommy guns to get on board and shoot me."

"Boy," Boo said gently, "I wouldn't let nobody shoot you. I give you my solemn word on that."

"I take *your* word," said Weber, "but I just can't take theirs. They've broken it too many times already. No, the sooner we take off, the sooner we'll be on Okinawa, and they've got good Army hospitals there and they'll take care of her. So please don't torment me, because there just isn't anything I can do."

"I guess not," said the musician. He yawned. "Man, I don't know how you do it. My tail is dragging."

"These," said the young soldier, holding up a small vial. "What's that?"

"Benzedrine," said Weber. Then, quickly, "I told you that before, didn't I? Why don't you listen?"

"It wasn't me," said Boo Brown. "I think you told the Captain."

"Oh," said the soldier. "Maybe you're right. What do you think of him, anyway? Do you think he's a good commander? I don't mean just a garrison commander, but a field man."

Carefully Boo replied, "I think he's probably one of the best. I admired him for the way he put the passengers' safety before his own."

"Yes," Weber agreed, "he did, didn't he?"

The plane began to move, slowly at first, but steadily increasing in speed. The mighty jet engines whined and bit into the air, sluggishly, then with authority and strength.

Specialist Five Jerry Weber leaned back in his seat and gripped the arm rests.

"Here we go again," he whispered.

## THE TENTH HOUR

The takeoff was easier than the landing. O'Hara had to be careful to keep the plane between the twin rows of blue runway lights, but once the multiple wheels had left the ground, he trimmed the 707 to climb and in a matter of minutes he had come through the cloud layer and blue sky was all around them.

"Right now," O'Hara muttered, "I'd give my left foot for one of those new inertial guidance systems. Johnny, figure out our heading for Dutch Harbor. Let's see if you can still remember how to read a map."

He would get a course from Air Traffic too, but the Captain felt the need to keep his Flight Engineer busy. He did not like the man's nervousness.

In the passenger compartments, all was still.

Boo Brown and Jerry Weber sat sipping from plastic glasses. The pistol was out of sight, and to a casual observer they were merely two friends having a quiet conversation.

Jenny O'Hara talked with Lovejoy Welles at the lounge table. Both girls looked frightened.

In the Tourist Compartment, Angela Shaw crouched in the aisle, holding Harriet Stevens' hand. The pregnant woman seemed to be without pain now, and both Angela and Congressman Lindner, who sat across the aisle, hoped that the pains had only been false labor.

"It's hot," said Harriet.

Lindner got up. "I'll get something," he said. He went back to the galley and found a cloth. But, unable to figure out how to turn on the cold water, he decided to try the rear rest rooms. He opened the nearest one and started to enter. Then he drew back and said, "Whoops! Sorry, ma'am."

"That's all right," said Elly Brewster. "I guess it's time I came out anyway."

When Angie came forward with the coffee, O'Hara asked, "How's our little mother?"

"Better," the girl said. "We're hoping it was just the excitement."

"Well, keep me posted," said the Captain.

"Yes, sir," Angie said. "Incidentally, we've got a stowaway."

"A what?"

"A stowaway."

O'Hara frowned. "Oh. My daughter. I'd almost forgotten about her being on board."

"Nope," said Angie. "A Miss Elly Brewster, the girl who found the original hijack message."

"Why do you call her a stowaway? Maybe she either couldn't or wouldn't get off."

Angie smiled. "It's how she got *on* in New York. She

141

pulled the oldest trick in the world—got hold of a blank envelope and made out her own boarding pass. That got her past the gate."

"How did she get on the plane?"

"Somebody goofed, I guess. I suppose she came on with a gang of people, waved her envelope at us, said, 'I know where my seat is' and hid out in the john until we'd finished counting heads. That's where we just found her. She meant to wait until we were all off the plane, then sneak off later. But she didn't get out in time."

"Well," said O'Hara, "I hope she enjoys her flight."

"You see," Elly Brewster explained to Congressman Lindner, "I just had to get to Seattle. My boy friend was shipping out, and I wasn't answering his letters for a while, and I couldn't let him go overseas without knowing that I wasn't really mad at him. I know it's corny, but I guess I have this thing for him after all."

"Why didn't you telephone?"

"I tried, but he wouldn't talk to me."

Lindner smiled, shaking his head gently. "Well, the way it looks," he told her, "you're going to be overseas before he is."

"Jeff's father will be awful mad at him," Jenny O'Hara told Lovejoy Welles. "And it's all my fault."

"I would have been terrified," Lovejoy said.

"I was," Jenny admitted. "First, we almost got hit by this big thing, and then when we got down on the runway, there it was ahead of us blocking everything. Jeff had to turn into the mud, and ripped off the landing gear and tore up the bottom of the fuselage." She touched the bloody clot on her head. "I stuck my head through the

142

omni indicator and broke it, I guess. Jeff didn't get a scratch, but I bet his father tears him up good."

"Oh!" cried Lovejoy. She had not noticed the girl's wound until now. She sprang up. "I'll get the first aid kit," she said. "Don't go anywhere."

"Where would I be going?" Jenny asked.

"There they are!" Allen Ross exalted. He pointed. Several thousand feet below and a mile ahead, Flight 901 was climbing out of a bank of white, fluffy clouds. "Get closer, get closer."

"I'll get as close as I legally can," said the pilot. He hoped that once these madmen got their pictures they would decide to return to Boise. He had served briefly on Adak years ago and had no burning desire to revisit that barren Aleutian island.

Ross ran back to the main cabin. "Get ready, get ready," he shouted. "We're coming up on them."

The two cameramen aimed their lenses.

"How about me?" asked the sound man. "What do you want me to do?"

"Let me have the mike," Ross said, "I'll ad lib a narration. Hey, hey! Look! There it is!"

"Sometimes I'd get so mad at my father," said Jerry Weber. "I mean, when I'd come home from school with a bloody nose, he'd just look at me and maybe tell me to go wash my face. He didn't seem to care who hit me, or whether I won the fight or lost it. He just didn't listen to anything I said."

"That don't mean he didn't care," Boo said. "Some men keep everything shut up inside. They feel things, but they just don't show them."

"Maybe," Weber said tonelessly. "Hey, look at that!" He was pointing at Lovejoy Welles, returning to the lounge with a large box with a red cross stenciled on its side. "Miss, where are you going with that first aid kit?"

Frightened, she said, "It's Captain O'Hara's daughter. She hurt her head in that plane crackup."

"That little girl?" Weber said, amazed. "Boy, I said she was a spunky one. Here, let me give you a hand. I had six weeks of first aid training. I almost became a Corpsman."

He took the box and went forward. Lovejoy remained near Boo, obviously flustered.

"Go on up and help," Boo Brown said gently. "He ain't so bad if you treat him like you would any other boy his age."

When Lovejoy got to the lounge, she found Weber examining Jenny's head with fingers that were gentle and sensitive as he parted the blood-clotted hair. His voice was low and soothing.

"These scalp wounds bleed a lot," he said, "but they don't amount to much. You're lucky, Miss O'Hara. If that was a couple of inches lower, you might have had a scar, but as it is, the cut's under the hair and it'll grow right over. I'm afraid I'm going to have to cut a little off now, though. You can't have hair and glass in a wound. It'll get infected."

"Can I help?" Lovejoy asked.

"Have you got a flashlight?"

"Yes." She took it from the rack over the main hatch.

"Hold it right here, so I can see good. That's it." He made delicate snips with the scissors. The matted hair fell to the formica top of the lounge table. Once, Jenny drew her breath in sharply. "Gosh, I'm sorry!" Weber said. "I'll

144

try to be more careful." He snipped some more, then put the scissors down. Their tips were dark with dried blood. "Okay," he said. "Now, Jenny, I'm going to have to clean that wound out because there's all kinds of dirt and junk in there. It'll sting. Maybe pretty bad. I'm sorry. This kit doesn't have anything to deaden the pain."

"Go ahead," she said. "I know you won't hurt me."

"I'll try not to," he promised.

He wet a swab with alcohol and began to cleanse the cut. Jenny's lips tightened, but she did not wince or make a sound.

"What the hell is that?" Sam Allen yelled, pointing through the right flight deck window.

O'Hara leaned over and squinted. "My God," he said, "it's another 707."

"I think it's chasing us," Sam told him. "Look, it's moving in closer."

O'Hara grabbed up the microphone. "Unidentified 707," he broadcast, "this is Trans-America 901. Who are you? What do you want?"

The answer came back immediately. "901, this is Charter 242. I have press aboard, and they're taking pictures of you."

"Jesus!" exploded O'Hara, "Are you all insane? Don't you know what will happen if he sees another plane moving in on us? Sheer off! You're endangering this flight and everyone aboard it."

The other plane began to climb as its pilot's voice came back, "I'm going upstairs, Captain, so your passengers can't see us. Is that acceptable?"

O'Hara grumbled a little, but he knew the predicament

the other pilot was in. "Okay," he said, "but stay out of sight."

Miles behind them, an Air Force Vindicator made an instrument landing at McCord Air Force Base and began taxiing toward the Operations Building.

"Sorry it didn't work out, sir," said the pilot.

Paul Manchester shrugged and stared out at the fog.

**THE ELEVENTH HOUR**

Vancouver Island was far behind them now, as were the Queen Charlotte Islands and the mainland of North America. The ocean below was a deep, aching blue, chilled by the Subarctic Current. In the event of a forced landing in such water, the life expectancy of a human being was less than five minutes before exposure and cold claimed their victim.

On orders from O'Hara, both Bimonte and Sam Allen were dozing, their neckties off and collars open. Flight 901 was on autopilot and, with favoring winds, was doing better than six hundred miles an hour ground speed.

There had been no interruptions from the passenger cabin for quite some time. O'Hara found himself hoping that the hijacker had gone to sleep. Not that he would sanction any attempt to disarm the man: it was more prudent to continue as instructed. After all, so far only man-hours and kerosene were being wasted.

At the lounge table Jerry Weber, Boo Brown, Jenny O'Hara, and Lovejoy Welles were playing penny poker.

Elly Brewster sat with Congressman Arne Lindner, across from the dozing Harriet Stevens. She was telling him about life in the East Village, and he listened in fascination. It reminded him of the year he had spent on San Francisco's North Beach before he had enlisted for the Korean War.

Angela Shaw foraged through all the compartments in both galleys to find enough food to put together some kind of meal for the remaining passengers and crew. When Lovejoy tried to help, Angie had told her it was more important to keep the young soldier's mind off the flight and on such trivials as penny poker.

High above them, out of sight of anyone aboard Flight 901, the chartered press plane flew. There had been some initial complaints from Allen Ross, but the charter pilot told him flatly that he would not endanger the hijacked plane by coming closer.

At McCord Air Force Base, Paul Manchester sipped coffee with the Vindicator's pilot. "Where are you off to next?" Paul asked.

The pilot shrugged. "I'm a free agent," he said. "In case we lost all our command facilities at Omaha and Stone Mountain, we're supposed to become free lance raiders. I may head down the coast, pull a surprise run on Los Alamos. That ought to shake them up."

Above their heads, the Officers' Club TV set flickered and an announcer appeared with "latest news about the hijacked Trans-America plane."

"That nut'll blow us up," John Bimonte said.

"No he won't," said O'Hara. "Goddammit, Johnny,

148

don't argue with me. I said to start dumping fuel. Do it."

"No," said the Flight Engineer.

O'Hara stared at him. "I'm in command of this plane," he said. "I told you to dump fuel from number two and number three tanks."

"And I said no," Bimonte answered steadily. "That kid isn't right in his head. If he finds out you've tricked him again, he'll stuff that grenade down your throat and pull the pin."

Five minutes before, Angela Shaw had pushed her way onto the flight deck and said, "Captain, we've got troubles. That woman's going to give birth any moment."

"Oh, Christ," O'Hara had answered. "I hope the Congressman is a good midwife."

She shook her head. "It's not that simple," Angie said. "She's bleeding. Badly."

"Okay," said O'Hara. "Do what you can. I'll get us on the ground."

"Anchorage is the nearest," Sam supplied.

"Thanks," O'Hara said. "Anchorage Operations," he broadcast, "this is Trans-America 901. Request clearance for emergency landing. Over."

"901, this is Anchorage," a voice replied. "Captain, we're socked in here so tight you couldn't pry your way in with a shoehorn. Fairbanks is open. Can you make it that far?"

"Affirmative," O'Hara said. "Sam, what's the frequency of Fairbanks Operations?"

Before Allen could look it up in the Flight Handbook, another voice came on the circuit. "901, this is Fairbanks. Anchorage has us patched into their frequency. What is the nature of your emergency and what is your ETA?"

"We have a pregnant woman on board," said O'Hara.

"She is in labor and bleeding badly. Request ambulance and medical assistance on the ramp. Our ETA"—he looked over at Sam Allen, who had scribbled on a pad—"is one hour and four minutes from now. Over."

"Roger," said Fairbanks. "Is there any further information?"

"Inform the officials that I am dumping fuel to make this landing appear necessary," O'Hara said. "But I have a hijacker aboard who wants to go to Okinawa. We may have to refuel in a hurry."

"Received and understood," said the voice. "Good luck, sir."

Now, when O'Hara ordered John Bimonte to begin draining the fuel from the wing tanks, the Flight Engineer refused.

"Johnny," O'Hara tried again, "it's the only thing we can do. That woman back there could die."

"If Junior sets off his grenade, we'll all die," Bimonte said. "Boss, you're wrong this time."

Grimly O'Hara said, "Sam, get back there and dump that fuel."

"Yes, Captain," Sam Allen said, looking directly at Bimonte as he said it.

"Word has just been received," said the TV announcer, "that the hijacked plane is now proceeding to Fairbanks, Alaska. The pregnant woman aboard has taken a turn for the worse, and the pilot has decided to dump fuel to force a landing there. The chartered 707 chase plane, carrying several of our ATC reporters and cameramen has confirmed the change in course. We hope to have films of the hijacked plane in flight and its landing in

150

Fairbanks in a matter of hours. Until then, stay tuned to ATC, Channel 12."

Paul Manchester looked at the pilot. "Would your orders let you head for Fairbanks instead of Los Alamos?" he asked.

"Let's go," said the pilot.

In Newark, New Jersey, Harriet Stevens' mother was frozen in front of the television set. Her husband sat near her, silent.

"I told her not to go," the woman said. "I told her over and over that something might happen."

"It's nobody's fault," said the man. "It's God's will."

Harvey Brandt, who had been relieved of his post at Cleveland Control after the wearying hours spent in communication with 901, sat in a downtown bar and stared at a color TV set over the cash register. He had been drinking beer, but now he waved at the bartender and said, "Lennie, give me a double bourbon."

Pouring a Wild Turkey, the bartender said, "That's some thing up there, ain't it? Boy, you're never going to get me off the ground in one of them things. You heard the story, didn't you? If God had wanted jet airplanes to fly, he'd have given them propellers."

"I heard it," Harvey said wearily.

In Fairbanks, William Reading's telephone rang at last. It was the District Director.

"Bill," said the Director, "we just got word, that hijacked plane is coming in here at Eielson Air Force Base in around an hour. Better get out there."

151

"I'm on my way," said the young FBI man.

"And, Bill," said the Director, "I understand you've got a good long range telescopic rifle."

"Pretty good," Reading said.

"Better bring it," the Director told him.

"Fairbanks?" yelled Marion Hotchkiss. "Get on the horn. Line up a hospital room, the best doctors, you know what to do. That poor woman."

"I'm on my way," said Herbert Kean.

"Two and three empty," said Sam Allen.

"Good," O'Hara replied. "Okay, Sam. You'd better get up here and fly this thing. I've got to go back and tell our young friend we don't have enough fuel to get anywhere but Fairbanks."

"How are you going to explain that?" asked Sam.

"They didn't fill us up in Seattle," O'Hara answered. "What else can I say?

He did not have to say anything. The cabin door opened and Jerry Weber came in.

"Captain," he said, "that woman back there's sicker than I thought. I've been trying to help her, but I didn't get that kind of training."

The young soldier's hands, O'Hara saw with a wave of nausea, were covered with fresh blood.

"I was just coming back to talk to you," O'Hara began.

"No time for talk," Weber said. "You've got to put this thing down. Right now. Where's the nearest airport?"

John Bimonte began to laugh. Weber swang around angrily. "What's the matter with him?" he almost shrieked.

"Nothing's the matter with me," said the Flight Engi-

152

neer. "Fairbanks. That's the nearest place to land. Fairbanks!"

"Okay," Weber said to O'Hara. "Fairbanks. Don't screw
around. That woman needs help. *Move!*"

# THE TWELFTH HOUR

Operations instructed O'Hara to land at Eielson Air Force Base rather than the Fairbanks commercial airport because the base hospital was only two minutes from the ramp. The approach of Flight 901 was uneventful. The weather was good and the skies clear.

An ambulance and two doctors waited, standing at the foot of the ramp with emergency medical equipment stacked in a wire basket that could be carried on board the aircraft if necessary.

In the Operations Office, a cluster of FBI men held a hurried conference. William Reading was there, with three other agents and the District Director. As the smallest, Reading had been selected to make another attempt to get aboard the hijacked plane through the flight deck's emergency hatch. He had been practicing on a KC-135, the Air Force version of the 707, and was confident he could slip into the hatch silently.

Downstairs, in the pilot's lounge, Paul Manchester drank brandy-laced coffee with the Vindicator's commander. The Air Force fighter-bomber had landed minutes before, after a record-breaking flight from Tacoma, Washington. For the last five hundred miles, the pilot had switched in the afterburners, consuming fuel at more than double the usual rate, but increasing the plane's speed by four hundred miles an hour.

"What are you going to do now, sir?" asked pilot.

"I'm not sure," Manchester said. "I've been worrying about getting here so hard that I didn't stop to consider what I'd do next."

"I heard, up in Operations," the pilot said, "that they're asking for volunteer pilots to spell O'Hara and his crew. They want guys with overwater rating, in case the plane goes on to Okinawa as they've indicated."

"I haven't touched a throttle in ten years," said Manchester.

"Maybe not," said the pilot, "but how are you with one of these?"

Silently he pushed a small, flat .38 caliber survival pistol across the table.


"I'm sorry to be so much trouble," Harriet Stevens said weakly. "It was foolish of me to travel in my condition."

"You couldn't know," Angie said softly. The woman's pulse felt weak and thready beneath her fingers. The bleeding had stopped, but Harriet's temple was bathed with cold perspiration.

Jerry Weber returned from the aft galley where he had washed his hands. He carried a steaming cup of tea.

"Try this," he said gently. "It'll make you feel better."

Harriet smiled at him. She sipped the tea slowly. "Are

155

you really a hijacker?" she asked.

Angela stiffened, but Weber did not react.

"Some might say that," he said. "But I just did what I had to do. Don't let it worry you none, ma'am. We'll have you to a doctor soon. You just lie quiet."

"You remind me of my husband," she said. "He's very quiet and gentle. Isn't it too bad that all you boys have to go off to war? What's wrong with us, anyway? I can't remember any moment in my life when we haven't been worrying about war and killing. That's not the way it was supposed to be."

"No, ma'am," said Weber, "it sure isn't."

"I'm sorry, Mike," said John Bimonte. "I went yellow on you."

O'Hara did not answer.

"I honestly believed you were wrong," the Flight Engineer continued. "Maybe it's different, serving as an enlisted man, like I did. But in Korea, I saw dozens like this kid. You couldn't trust them for a minute. They're unpredictable."

"Johnny," said Sam Allen.

"Yeah?"

"Please shut up."

Flight 901 appeared over the south boundary of Eielson Air Force Base. Flaps extended, landing gear groping down toward the waiting concrete, it settled onto the runway.

Inside, Jerry Weber went forward to the flight deck.

"Captain," he said, "I'm sorry for all the trouble I've caused you, but I've got to tell you, I won't sit still for any tricks. We landed to let a sick woman off, and then we're going on."

"We have to refuel," said O'Hara. "We didn't take on a full load in Seattle."

"I think I've changed my mind about Okinawa," Weber said. "Nobody's going to listen to me, not even a combat commander. I'm a pirate. That's what they call hijacking, isn't it? Aerial piracy? And the punishment is death. Or worse, they'd lock me up for the rest of my life."

"Jerry," O'Hara said earnestly, "it isn't as bad as you think. We want to help you. Nobody's going to railroad you. What you've done just now will help you. Do yourself a favor. End it right here. I swear I'll testify in your behalf."

"I know you would, Captain," said the young soldier, "but I just can't take the chance. Get this thing filled up with fuel. And you'd better start working on our new course."

Wearily O'Hara asked, "Where's that, son?"

"Moscow," said Specialist Five Jerome Weber, nervously clicking the reloaded cylinder of his revolver.


"I can fake him out as a Flight Engineer," Paul Manchester said desperately. He was speaking with the District Director of the FBI.

"You're a civilian," said the FBI man. "We can't take the risk."

"Do any of your men know how to fly an airplane?" Manchester demanded.

"No, but—"

"That kid out there is sharp. You don't think he's going to let a bunch of strangers get on board without checking them out, do you? Listen, I'm rusty, but I can fly, and I know my way around a flight deck. I'm your best bet."

157

"I agree," said the District Director, after a pause. "I just wish there were some other way."

"Don't worry, I'm not going to take any stupid risks," Manchester said. "My—the girl I'm going to marry is on that plane."

"Good luck," said the FBI man.

"How about the rest of the people on board?" O'Hara asked. "There's no reason why you shouldn't let them get off here."

"It's all right with me," Weber said. "But no tricks." He was sitting in the open door between the flight deck and the cabin. "Go ahead, announce it, but nobody except the doctor gets on or I'll release this lever." He had pulled the pin from the grenade again, this time placing it carefully in his breast pocket.

"No tricks," O'Hara promised. His voice, amplified by the loudspeaker system, said, "Attention, please. I have been informed that it is permissible for all remaining passengers to leave the aircraft. Please deplane by the forward hatch. Angie and Lovejoy, it'd be nice if one of you stayed to rustle up the coffee and sandwiches. We've still got a little distance to go. Jenny, I want you to get off. As soon as you get in the terminal, call your mother. She must be worried."

Sweating, he replaced the microphone in its cradle.

"Mike," John Bimonte said softly.

"What?"

"You don't need me anymore. Can I get off too?"

O'Hara cursed.

After another argument, the FBI was persuaded not to try shooting out the 707's tires. "Jesus," muttered O'Hara, "they've got a one-track mind about those damned snipers."

The District Director knew, however, that William Reading had already crept into the emergency hatch beneath the flight deck. Reading decided to wait until the aircraft was in the air to penetrate into the cabin; by then, he reasoned the hijacker would have returned to the passenger cabin. He reached up and secured an open latch; now no one would look down accidentally and see him.

Supplies of food and liquor were brought on board. Jerry Weber did not permit the caterers to come onto the airplane. The containers were stacked in the main hatch. Sam Allen came back and dragged them inside.

Weber did permit the two doctors to come on board to examine Harriet Stevens. They placed her in a stretcher and carried her to the hatch where a fork lift waited to lower them to the ground. At the door she turned to Weber, sitting in the entrance to the flight deck.

"Thank you," she said.

Weber gave a vague motion of his head and looked away.

"Jerry," O'Hara called to him, "Sam and I are worn out. What's more, we don't have any Polar flight experience. I want to bring on an alternate crew to help out."

"You're the Captain," Jerry said. "I don't want anyone else."

"I'll remain in charge," O'Hara assured him. "But I need help."

Considering, Weber said finally, "Okay. But no tricks."

Carefully, three men climbed aboard. One wore an Air Force uniform. The other two were in civilian clothes.

"Are you the standby crew?" Weber asked, holding the

grenade out in front of him.

"Yes," said the uniformed man. "Don't worry, we're not going to do anything but help Captain O'Hara fly this airplane."

Weber moved aside. Slowly the three men filed onto the flight deck. Behind them, Angela Shaw, who had decided to remain aboard in response to O'Hara's request, gasped.

The last man in line was Paul Manchester. He looked at her, no recognition showing in his eyes.

"How are you, Stewardess?" he asked.

William Reading huddled in the tiny compartment beneath the flight deck. The metal ribs of the bare structure bit into his back and thighs. He felt the aircraft trembling as men moved around above him.

It was going to be a long wait.

In the darkness he pressed his hand against the cold steel of the .38 Police Special.

Sam Allen slammed the main hatch closed and dogged it down tightly. In the jump seat nearby, John Bimonte sat sullenly.

"What are you looking at me for?" he demanded, as Sam glanced down at him. "What am I supposed to be, some kind of hero? You don't need me. Why should I have to stay on board?"

"Don't ask me, Johnny," Sam said. "As far as I'm concerned, we'd be better off without you."

"Some friend," Bimonte grumbled.

Sam Allen shrugged and went back to his position on the flight deck.

"You know," Jerry Weber said softly, "in combat they'd shoot you."

Bimonte stared at the dogged-down hatch and said nothing.

"Go back to the rear," Weber said. "I don't want to look at you." Bimonte did not react. Weber stood up and yelled, "*Move!*"

John Bimonte rose and staggered back to the Tourist Compartment. He was mumbling to himself.

Weber went forward. He stood on the crowded flight deck and looked at the five men clustered around the controls.

"So you're all pilots," he said. "Well, before we take off you're going to have to prove it."

"Jerry," said O'Hara, "it's almost 4200 miles to Moscow. And what's more, we're not even sure the Soviets will let us penetrate their air space. That's what I'm doing now, trying to get clearance. Will you please give me another couple of minutes on the radio?"

"Okay," said Weber. "But make it fast."


"Where are they?" Allen Ross grumbled, sitting in the forward compartment of the rented 707 at Fairbanks Airport.

"They should have been in by now," said the sound man.

Ross glared at Happy Gunther. "It was your idea to get ahead of them so we could film the landing from the ground," he complained.

"Well, we are ahead of them," the cameraman said. "When they come in we'll get them."

The pilot, who had come back from the flight deck,

stood over them and smiled. "Sorry, boys," he said, not bothering to conceal his delight, "it looks like you struck out. They landed over at Eielson Air Force Base. They're taking off in five minutes for Moscow."

Ross leaped up. "You didn't tell me there were two airports up here!" he yelled.

"You didn't ask. It was logical that they should have landed here, being a civilian plane. But somebody had another idea."

"Well, let's get going," Ross said.

The pilot shook his head. "Nope," he said. "I've been in touch with the home office. Your charter is terminated, right here. You live a little too rich for our blood."

Ross cursed, threatened, cajoled, to no avail. "Okay," he said finally, accepting the inevitable, "take us back to Boise."

"Not me, buddy," said the pilot. "There's a commercial flight at midnight to Seattle. If you've got enough cash, maybe you can get on it. As far as I'm concerned, you're offloaded. Lots of luck, fellows. Bad luck, if you get my meaning."


Flight 901 was ready to take off again. It waited for clearance on the end of the runway.

Huddled in the emergency exit beneath the flight deck, FBI man William Reading felt the powerful vibration of the engines. His head ached and there was a void in the pit of his stomach.

On the flight deck, the tension had relaxed somewhat after the performance test Jerry Weber had put the new men through.

"You!" he had told the uniformed man, "Start up those left-hand engines out there."

162

"Sure," said the new pilot. He bent forward and adjusted the fuel mixture, the throttles, then fired up the two port engines.

"Okay," Weber said to one of the other two men, "you get the others going."

The second man made some careful movements and all four engines were whining.

"All right," Weber said to Paul Manchester. "Now it's your turn. Get this baby moving."

"I can't reach the foot controls from here," Manchester said. "Is it all right if I tell Captain O'Hara what to do?"

"Go ahead."

"Captain," Manchester said, "throttles half forward."

"Half forward," O'Hara repeated, obeying.

"Use your toe brakes to turn the aircraft," Manchester said.

Sam Allen shut his eyes. You do not turn a 707 with toe brakes.

"Roger," said O'Hara. "Turning."

He made an obvious show of manipulating brakes with his feet. But his left hand was using the nose wheel control to steer the plane.

"Manifold Pressure check," said Manchester. Allen winced again. Jet engines do not have manifold gauges.

"Ninety over forty," O'Hara replied.

"Good," said Manchester. "Do you have your tower clearance?"

"Affirmative," said O'Hara.

"Let's get moving then," said the advertising man.

"That's good enough," said Jerry Weber. "You heard what the man said, Captain. Let's get this thing off the ground."

"Okay, Jerry," said O'Hara, sweat running down his

forehead into his eyes.

With almost sixty thousand pounds of thrust bursting from the four jet engines, the huge plane trembled at the end of the runway.

"Full forward on the yoke," called Captain Michael O'Hara, and the 707 began to move.

# THE THIRTEENTH HOUR     EST

The flight distance from Fairbanks, Alaska, to Moscow is almost exactly 4100 miles, directly over the North Pole. Leaving Eielson Air Force Base, O'Hara would cross the Arctic Circle in less than a hundred miles, as he flew over the village of Beaver. From there to the coast of the Beaufort Sea was another twenty minutes, and then for two thousand miles there would be only pack ice and glaciers below.

After crossing the Pole, the 707 would continue over the Barents Sea, past Murmansk and Leningrad and on into Moscow.

Estimated flight time was six and a half hours.

So far, Trans-America had not received clearance from the Soviet Union to penetrate that nation's air space, although Canada had granted permission to overfly its portion of the Arctic wasteland. O'Hara pointed out the lack of response from the Soviets to Jerry Weber.

"Don't worry about it," the young soldier said. "Even if they send up fighter planes, they'll see we're an unarmed commercial plane."

"They may shoot first and look later," said O'Hara. "It wouldn't be the first time. And what if they use missiles? Jerry, they may not let us cross their coastline."

"We'll worry about that when the time comes," Weber said. "I'm going back and get some coffee. Anyone want some?"

"Black," said O'Hara. "How about you guys?"

The three newcomers, crowded into the small cabin, declined. "I'll give you a hand," Sam Allen offered.

"I've got a better idea than that," Weber said. "These guys came on board to work. Let them do the flying for a while. You two come back and relax. Do you play poker?"

"Cut throat," said Allen.

There was much crowding as seats were changed. The uniformed pilot took the left seat, the other civilian the right, and Paul Manchester slid into the Flight Engineer's slot.

"Wait a minute," called the new pilot. "Captain, there's a weather message for you."

O'Hara started to say, "You take it," but the look in the man's eye stilled his voice. He slipped on the headphones.

"O'Hara here," he said. "Go ahead."

"This is Fairbanks Control," said a voice. "I've got the District Director of the FBI here. He says it's urgent that he speak with you."

"Fine," said O'Hara. "What are the conditions over the North Pole?"

"Captain," said a new voice, "has Reading been able to get into your cabin yet?"

"Reading?" said O'Hara. "No, I don't think that's on our route."

"We've got a man named Bill Reading on board your plane," the FBI Director said grimly. "He's in the emergency compartment underneath your seat. You've got to let him in before you reach cruise altitude or he'll die from cold and lack of oxygen."

O'Hara's lips tightened. "Dammit," he said, "you should have checked with me first!" He looked at the altimeter. "We've been at cruise altitude for five minutes. He's probably dead already. What are you, a bunch of idiots?"

"It's too late for recriminations," was the answer from Fairbanks. "Captain, you've got to do something."

"I'll do what I can," O'Hara said. He reached over and switched off the radio. "Jerry," he said softly, "they tried to screw us up."

"Who?" the young soldier demanded.

"The FBI. They smuggled someone on board."

Paul Manchester stiffened. His hand crept toward the .38 pistol which had been concealed in the small of his back when he boarded. Weber had patted the three men down, but missed the tiny pistol.

Before Manchester could make a desperate move, doomed to inevitable failure because Weber had his own pistol cocked and ready, O'Hara continued, "They slipped a man into an emergency hatch down there, beneath my seat."

Weber swore. "You promised there wouldn't be any tricks," he said.

"And there won't be," O'Hara answered. "I didn't put that agent down there. He may already be dead—there's almost no oxygen and it's fifty below in that hatch. But I promise you, if he's alive, I'll make sure he's disarmed and, if you insist, we'll tie him up or lock him in one of the rest rooms."

"The hell with him," said Weber. "He can't get up here unless you let him?"

"We have to move my seat," O'Hara replied.

"Let him stay where he is. I don't want anyone else on this plane."

"Jerry," O'Hara said gently, "we can't do that. He'll freeze to death or die from lack of oxygen."

"That's his problem," Weber said.

O'Hara shook his head. "You don't want murder on your conscience," he said. "I know what kind of man you are, Jerry. I don't blame you for being mad. I'm mad myself. They put something over on both of us. But that's not enough reason to let a man die."

Weber hesitated. "Okay," he said. "But remember I'm standing here." He pressed the pistol against Paul Manchester's head. "Maybe I won't be able to get your FBI man before he gets me, but I can sure blast this one."

"Don't worry," O'Hara said. "He'll come up out of there with his hands in the air." He fumbled the seat aside and bent over the hatch. After a moment he straightened, sweating.

"What's wrong?" asked Weber.

"I can't get it open," said the pilot. "He must have locked it from the inside."


"What *is* this?" Angela Shaw demanded. "A stowaway's convention? You were supposed to get off!"

"I couldn't leave Daddy," Jenny O'Hara said. "He needs me."

"And what about you?" Angie demanded. "Is he your Daddy too?"

168

Boo Brown grinned and spread his hands. "Like," he said, "my ticket read San Francisco. I wasn't about to get off with those Eskimos out there. You know what they do on these cold winter nights? They lend you their wives."

Angie tried to suppress a smile. "So?"

Boo shivered. "Have you ever seen an Eskimo wife? No, ma'am!" His voice lowered. "Besides," he said softly, "me and that boy get along. Maybe me being here will make the difference between him behaving or doing something stupid. And besides, I gave him my solemn word nobody'd hurt him."

Angela raised her eyes to the cabin roof. "You're all insane," she said. "I don't know what gets into people."

Jenny got up. "I can cook," she said, then corrected, "at least, a little. Let me help you."

"Why not?" Angela said. "What *else* can happen?"

"We can't take her down," O'Hara said. "If we do, we won't have fuel enough to make Russia." He had a heavy screwdriver and a hammer, and was trying to force the hatch lock.

"Even if you get that thing open," warned Sam Allen, "we might have an explosive decompression on our hands."

"I don't think so," said O'Hara. "The outside hatches are closed. Whatever pressure differential there is between us and the compartment won't make much difference."

"It better not," said Allen.

"Goddammit!" said O'Hara, his voice almost breaking under the strain, "What the hell do you want me to do? Let the poor bastard die?" He hit at the base of the screwdriver, missed and smashed his thumb and cursed again.

"You're going at it all wrong," said Weber. "Let me have it."

He pushed the pilot aside, wedged the screwdriver into one corner of the hatch and tapped gently. "Slow and easy," he said. "You don't get anything open with force. Just like—so!" and as he said "So," there was a snapping sound and the hatch fell open with a slight whooshing sound.

O'Hara forgot his throbbing thumb and pressed forward to help Weber pull the limp figure up from the cramped area beneath the seat.

"Is he alive?" Sam Allen asked anxiously.

"I don't know," said O'Hara. And to the eye it appeared that William Reading was beyond help. His hair was white with frost; his face was bluish and his eyes stared. Weber pressed his thumb against the FBI man's throat.

"There's a pulse," he said. "Another five minutes, though, and we just might as well have left him down there." The young soldier stepped back. "Does he have a gun?" he asked.

"Here it is," O'Hara said, handing Weber Reading's .38 Police Special.

"Goddammit!" Weber exploded. "Why don't they listen to me? I ought to shoot this bastard right now." He raised the pistol and pointed it at the unconscious FBI man. "That'd teach them to get the wax out of their ears."

O'Hara stepped between them. "Don't do it, Jerry," he said.

Weber hesitated. "Okay," he said. "Take him back to the tail and lock him up. Where's that chicken Flight Engineer of yours? Put him in charge of this prisoner. Tell him if this guy gets loose, I'll shoot them both. That ought to keep him on his toes. Come on, get him out of here!"

As O'Hara and Sam Allen carried the limp FBI man back Allen muttered, "He's right on the edge, Mike."

"I know it," O'Hara said. "This idiot almost put him over."

As they passed the little group in First Class, he glared at his daughter. "I told you to get off," he said.

She looked down at the floor. "I'm sorry, Daddy."

"Who's that cat?" asked Boo Brown.

O'Hara explained. The musician whistled. "Man," he said, "don't they have any better sense than that? This kid's only going to take so much more pushing before he explodes like an A-bomb."

"Why don't I see if I can get him to come back here?" Angie asked. "He and Jenny got along pretty well. Maybe it'll calm him down again."

O'Hara started to say, "I don't want my daughter—" but then he stopped and looked down at Jenny with newly aware eyes. This was not the pug-nosed, skinned-kneed brat who had made his last vacation a yowling disaster. He saw, emerging from the little girl that had been, a young woman.

"Okay," he said, grunting under William Reading's weight. "Why not? It couldn't hurt."

Angela Shaw hurried forward as they carried the FBI man into the rear compartment.

John Bimonte waited for them uneasily. "Who's that?" he asked. "What's going on."

With some delight, Sam Allen explained Weber's instructions. "You can't keep him in one of the johns be-

171

cause they don't lock from the outside, but by God you'd better tie him up good and keep him back here because if that kid sees him again he's promised to shoot you both."

O'Hara returned to the First Class Compartment without comment. He felt sickened and dirtied by what had happened to Bimonte on this flight.

He sat down beside his daughter. "How's your mother?" he asked.

"Just like I told you," Jenny said. "I'm really worried about her."

"Once this is over," he said, "I'll take a few days off. Maybe we can help if we all try at once."

"I hope so, Daddy," she said softly.


"Permission denied," said the Soviet official from six thousand miles away. "Have you gotten tired of 'weather planes' straying off course, and now try to deceive us with a so-called 'hijacked' airliner? Our orders are to shoot down any aircraft without prior clearance, and this mysterious plane has no clearance at all."

The Eielson Air Force Base Operations Officer stopped the tape recorder. "That's it, sir," he said to Congressman Arne Lindner, who had just returned from the hospital to which Harriet Stevens was taken. "They're taking a very hard line. And they mean it, sir. They'll shoot that 707 right out of the sky."

"What about their higher authority? Any word from Moscow?"

"Not a peep, sir," said the Operations Officer. "This is highly unusual, as you know, and they're inclined to be very suspicious when procedures break down."

"But they must know this is a civilian aircraft."

"Sir, they know only what they want to know. And

172

right now they're not giving us any feedback whatsoever on our request to clear 901 for Moscow. They're taking the attitude that it's an unauthorized overflight, period."

"Something tells me," Lindner said, "that I am rapidly wearing out my welcome at the White House. But connect me anyway."

"They're still on board?" Jerry Weber said. "Why didn't they get off like I said?" He was standing on the flight deck behind the new pilot.

Angie shrugged. "Jenny wanted to stay with her father," she said. "And Mr. Brown told me he's got a date to play you some music."

Weber smiled. "See, *he* didn't forget what I said," he told her. "Did you ever hear him play?"

"Only on records."

"Maybe we'll have a concert over the North Pole. Wouldn't that be something? Sure, I'll go back with you and talk to them. I hope the Captain took my advice about resting. I don't mind these guys"—and he nodded at the three newcomers—"flying this thing, but there's only one man I'd trust to land us in Moscow."

He jammed Reading's pistol into his belt and stood up. "No tricks now, you hear?" he told the new pilot.

"Stewardess?" called the new Flight Engineer.

"Yes, sir?"

"Can I have some black coffee?"

"Right away."

She walked back with Weber. "How old are you?" he asked.

"That's not polite," she said. "No girl tells. Over twenty-one. All right?"

"I'm sorry," he said. "I didn't mean to be impolite. I

173

was just interested. I like you."

"I'm not angry," she said. "Do you want anything?"

"Could you make an egg sandwich?"

"I'm not sure what they put on board, but if we have eggs I can."

"That's what I'd like," he said. "I don't know what time it is, but I'm hungry as a wolf."

"I'll take the crew their coffee and get right on it," Angie said.

When she gave Paul Manchester his tray, she hissed, "What are *you* doing here? Are you some kind of nut?"

"I'm just protecting my investment," he said. "I've got a couple of thousand scoots tied up in a ring, remember?"

"Oh, you big lummox," she said, beginning to sob. He pulled her to him and held her tight.

"It's okay, baby," he said. "I'm here."

"But why? How?"

"It wasn't easy," he said, and told her about the Vindicator flight. "I'd owe the Air Force around fifty grand if I had to pay for charter service."

When he told her about the pistol, she shivered. "Oh, Paul," she said, "I hope it doesn't come to that. He's really not a bad boy."

"I hope it doesn't too," he said, "but that really not a bad boy has risked a hundred lives half a dozen times. And if you think I'm going to let him hurt you—"

"He wouldn't hurt me, darling," she said. "Please, don't do anything desperate."

"I won't," he promised. "Not unless it turns into a desperate situation."

"That was a great egg sandwich," Jerry Weber told Angie.

174

She dipped a curtsy. "Thank you," she said. "We aim to please."

"Do you play poker? We've got a fast game going here."

"Sorry," she said. "I never learned. Besides, I've got to start the coffee flowing to keep that gang up front awake."

He grinned, holding up a small vial. "They ought to have these," he said. "One every couple of hours and you never want to go to bed."

Her face was impassive. "What's the matter?" he asked.

"I don't like pills," she said.

"Oh, hell," he said, tossing them to her. "If it bothers you that much, flush them down the john. They're only Benzedrine."

She looked at the vial carefully. "Are you sure you want to give these to me?" she asked. "You might need them."

"I won't fall asleep," he said. Then, smiling up at her, "And if I did—you wouldn't let them hurt me, would you?"

Wordless, she whirled and ran back to the rear rest rooms and locked herself in one. Outside, John Bimonte lifted his head from a *Life* magazine and looked around, puzzled.

Beyond the door, he thought he heard deep, wracking sobs.

Back on the flight deck, O'Hara responded to the new pilot's wordless gesture toward the headphones and fastened them around his ears.

"O'Hara here," he said.

"Captain, this is Fairbanks Control. We have received

word that the Russian Air Command has issued orders to shoot down your aircraft if you violate Soviet air space. The President has been trying to reach the Soviet Premier on the hot line to request clearance for your overflight, but his attempts have failed so far. Can you turn back?"

"Negative," said O'Hara.

"Perhaps a message to the hijacker directly from the White House? I am told that the President himself suggested this."

"Thanks, but it wouldn't work," said O'Hara. "Listen, keep trying for that clearance. We've got plenty of time yet. And do me a favor."

"Anything, sir."

"Call Mrs. Michael O'Hara in Portland, Oregon. That's Area Code 503, and the number is 799-1454. Got that?"

"Yes, sir."

"Tell her Jenny is on board with me and everything is all right. I'll call her as soon as we land."

"Yes, sir."

"And, listen—"

"Yes, Captain?"

"Nothing," O'Hara said finally. "That's all. Thanks." He had been about to ask the Operations man not to tell Joyce where he was bound but decided it was foolish. The radio and TV stations would already be carrying the news.

"There's the coast," said the new pilot. "From here on in, it's Santa Claus country."

"Ho, ho, ho," said O'Hara, starting back to the passenger cabin.

## THE FOURTEENTH HOUR

Now the long time began. Where, decades before, men had sworn and frozen and endured the almost unbearable cold to beat their ways to the Pole, now the silver airplane flew high above the ice that was invisible except as a great, shimmering whiteness that might well have been low-lying clouds. Six miles beneath them, pack ice ground against itself, howling winds blasted the barren surface with the intensity of a wind tunnel, and there was not more than one human being in every hundred square miles to look up at the violently blue sky and wonder at the straight white lines of the jet's contrails.

Instead of flushing away the Benzedrine tablets, Angie had given them to O'Hara. He read the label carefully and then deliberately swallowed one of the pills. "I'll pay for this tomorrow," he said. "These things only keep you from sleeping, they don't keep you from wanting to sleep."

"Why did he give them to you?" Sam Allen asked.

"He trusts me," the girl said. "I feel like a rat. I was supposed to throw them away."

"Listen, Angie," O'Hara said carefully, "the more alert we are, the better his chances. If we can keep him from doing something stupid, it'll be to his advantage too."

"I know that," she said. "It's just that—"

She could not finish. Instead, she went back to the galley and started preparing dinner.

"What's with our new Flight Engineer?" Sam asked.

"At first I thought he was FBI," O'Hara said. "But then I recognized him. He's Angie's boy friend. Don't ask me how he got up to Fairbanks, or how he got on board, but here he is. I had to play along with him. But he and I are going to have a little talk some time soon."

And as he spoke, the Boeing 707 bored its way through the thin air another three miles closer to Moscow.

As it did, Soviet radar operators huddled over their greenish scopes and watched the progress of the tiny white blip, moving ever nearer to the fighter planes that were already hooked up to the starting carts.

178

P.M.

EST

## THE FIFTEENTH HOUR

O'Hara came back to the poker game at the lounge table. He touched Jerry Weber on the shoulder.

"Congratulations," he said. "You're a godfather, or something."

"What do you mean?"

"Mrs. Stevens had her baby. A boy, eight pounds, three ounces. Mother and child doing well. She thought you might like to know."

Weber looked down at his cards, eyes blinking rapidly.

"Why would *I* want to know?" he mumbled.

O'Hara shrugged. "No reason. Who's winning?"

"She is," Weber said, nodding toward Jenny O'Hara. "She keeps drawing to inside straights and getting them." He looked up at O'Hara. "I hope it doesn't run in the family."

"Not me," O'Hara said. "I'm strictly a percentage man."

"Good," said Weber. "You want to sit in?"

179

"Not now. I'm going back to see how our stowaway is."

Weber swore, then said to Jenny, "Sorry." To O'Hara: "He's going to be all right, isn't he?"

O'Hara shrugged. "It depends on whether there was any brain damage from oxygen insufficiency. If he's unlucky, he might wind up as a vegetable."

"It's their own fault," Weber said. "Why did they have to sneak him in there? That's how guys get killed."

"I agree a hundred per cent," O'Hara said. He went back into the Tourist section.

"That's a good man," said the musician, studying his cards.

"He's a wonderful *pilot,*" Jenny said.

Weber looked at her. "He's your father," he said. "You're not supposed to talk against him."

"I wouldn't do that," she said. "But it's a whole life in itself, being a pilot. Your family almost never sees you. And it was worse, before the jets. I was just a little girl, but I still remember him being gone for four and five days at a time on trips." She put her cards on the table, face down. "I think I fold," she said.

"Yeah," Weber said, "I guess I never thought of it that way. It's kind of like being in the Army, isn't it? You go where the schedule takes you, and if you've got a family, that's just too bad."

"It's really bad when your family loves you and wants you near," the girl said. "Look, Jerry, this must be boring to you. Why don't I have Angie turn up the music? Do you dance?"

"I never tried," he said.

"You're putting me on! Everybody dances."

"I never tried," he repeated.

"Well, we'll fix that. You just stay right here." She hurried back to the galley.

"I wish I had a sister like that," Weber said. "I always wondered what it would be like to have a sister."

"About like having a wife," Boo said. "They take over your life, nag the daylights out of you, insist on being treated like one of the boys and when you do, they turn on the tears like a faucet. I know, I got three sisters."

"I'm an only child," Weber said. "My father treated me like I was a grown man from the time I was three years old. I never knew what being a kid was like. Maybe if I'd had a sister, we could have played together."

"Maybe," Boo said.

"Hey, when are you going to get out your cello for me? You promised, remember."

"I didn't forget," Boo answered. "Let's get some chow in us first, then I'll put on a little after-dinner concert. How does that grab you?"

"Crazy," said Weber. He repeated it, "Crazy!" and laughed.

"Man," Boo Brown said, "what are you going to do in Moscow?"

"Do?"

"I mean, why Moscow? You're not one of those reds or anything."

"Not me!"

"Then why do you want to go to Russia? You don't think those Ruskies are going to welcome you with open arms, do you? You know what happened to all those cats who hijacked planes to Cuba? Castro made them work twelve hours a day on the sugar cane plantations. Man, they were better off in the cotton fields."

"I didn't figure on doing anything in particular," Weber said. "Only, I don't know where else to go. I guess everything just went wrong. At first I thought if I could make that shipment, things would be all right. I've been in trouble before, I told you that, and they're just waiting to get me on something. So I had to make the shipment, you understand that. I don't know why the FBI had to make such a big fuss in Seattle. If they'd let me get off the plane and down to my outfit, that would have been the end of it with everybody happy. But they wouldn't listen and now look what's happened! That poor woman almost had her baby right here on this airplane, and the FBI man back there may have burned out his brain, and we're on our way to Russia and it's all their fault! They wouldn't leave me alone. If they wanted me to go to Moscow, they didn't have to go to all this trouble. They could have just given me a ticket and said, 'Get out.' I don't stay where I'm not wanted. But it makes me mad because I'm just as good an American as anyone, and it isn't my fault that first sergeant was down on me. Listen, where's my suitcase? If anybody's been fooling around with it—"

"You put it under the table," Boo said quietly. "I guess it's still there. I can feel something with my foot."

Weber bent down and looked. "I don't want nobody fooling with it," he said. "I've still got a few surprises if I need them."

Nervously Boo said, "I don't know about you, soldier boy, but my stomach is wrapped around my backbone. Why don't we have that nice girl serve up the chow?"

"That's fine with me," Weber answered. "I had an egg sandwich a while ago, but I'm still a little hungry."

Boo reached over and pressed the stewardess Call Button. In the galley a soft chime sounded.

Jenny O'Hara came back. "It'll be a while before we eat," she said. "Angie's found some beautiful steaks and she says this is the first time on any airplane that she's had time to cook them properly, so you're just going to have to wait because she isn't passing up this chance. But she's putting on some dance tapes, Jerry, and I'll give you a lesson."

"I'm not sure . . ." Weber said hesitantly.

"Come on," she said, holding out both hands. "Everybody has to start sometime."

The music began, softly at first, then louder as Angie turned up the master control. Jerry Weber clenched both hands in his lap and stared at the pile of playing cards.

"Well," said Jenny O'Hara, "what are you waiting for?"

Clumsily Weber reached out and took her hands in his.

"Nothing, I guess," he said, and got up.

"I messed it up," said William Reading.

"You sure did," O'Hara growled. "My God, don't you guys ever learn? Every time I put this plane down, there you were, gung ho for glory and the hell with the safety of my aircraft and its passengers."

"We were trying to insure your safety, not jeopardize it," said the young FBI man.

"Sure you were. Well, mister, you can thank God that you're sitting up here alive instead of being frozen down in that compartment like a side of beef. I'm sorry about having to tie you up, but that was the deal I made with the kid."

"You don't have to stick to any promise forced under duress," said Reading. "Listen, we can still take him. If I get close enough, I don't need weapons."

"Forget it, J. Edgar," said O'Hara. "I've got enough troubles. Why don't you relax and enjoy the scenery? Incidentally, do you have official identification on you?"

183

"Of course. It's a regulation."

"Well, if you want I'll tear it up and flush it down the john."

Reading started. "What the hell for?"

O'Hara gave him an evil smile. "It just occurred to me how delighted the Soviet secret police would be to get their hands on an FBI man."

Thirty-one thousand feet above the Arctic Ocean, a few hundred miles from the North Pole, Specialist Five Jerry Weber held Jenny O'Hara awkwardly in his arms and danced slowly to music by David Rose.

"See?" she said. "It isn't hard to do."

Sweating, Weber agreed, "No, I guess it isn't." She frowned and he asked, "What's wrong?"

She patted his waist and then his pocket. "These things," she said. "They make you feel all lumpy."

"Excuse me," he said, stepping away. He took both pistols and placed them on the lounge table. They lay on the formica near the playing cards, looking black and deadly. "Keep an eye on them for me, buddy," he told Boo Brown.

The musician looked at the weapons, inches away from his pudgy fingers. "I sure will," he said.

In the Ready Room of a Soviet air base just outside Leningrad, three fighter pilots finished their hot tea and studied charts of the approaches to the Russian coastline.

One, younger than the others, said, "Do you think it really *could* be an airliner?"

"Orders are orders," said the man nearest him. "Airliner or not, we shoot it down."

**THE SIXTEENTH HOUR**   E S T

Now, when we have learned to fling men at the stars, a flight across the polar regions is so commonplace that its route is not even mentioned in advertising or public relations handouts. Daily, dozens of aircraft crisscross back and forth over the frozen North, according to their destinations, without comment or scrutiny except by the ever-turning radar dishes of the Distant Early Warning network.

But Flight 901 had excited the interest of the world. It was plotted on television maps around the globe, as deep-voiced announcers speculated on its ultimate fate and as hastily recruited experts discoursed on the psychology of the hijacker. In New York a woman psychologist was rushed to a studio to give her opinion of the unknown psyche that bore the name of Jerome Weber. To her credit she did not attempt to probe his character by long distance but limited her comments to a profile of the classic hijacker personality.

In Chicago the expert was not so ethical. He spent some time discussing penis envy and the similarity of the flight and the womb experience. Few of his listeners understood one word out of ten, and all the announcer could say afterward was, "Thank you for a most enjoyable half hour." Since the psychologist had been on camera for less than five minutes, the announcer's confusion about time spoke volumes.

In New York, the *Call-Record* had gone through four Special Extras, and a fifth was on the presses. Reporters had called on Jerry Weber's father and while the man was being subjected to a bewildering interview by a by-line writer who kept asking him about Jerry's drinking habits, his companion stole a photograph of the boy from its frame on the mantlepiece. The only useful quote the elder Weber gave was, "He was always a good boy. I can't believe he'd do anything like this. He was always a little gentleman."

Ken Harper picked up the phrase, and the fifth extra's headline read: LITTLE GENTLEMAN FORCES JET TO MOSCOW.

"Your steak's going to get cold," Angie said.

Jerry Weber grinned. "Look, Ma," he said, "I'm dancing."

"What?" the stewardess asked.

"It's an old saying," Boo Brown told her.

"Well, come on and eat," she said. "I didn't slave over that hot galley so you could insult my cooking."

"Yes, ma'am," said Weber. He released Jenny O'Hara. "Wow, that was fun," he said. "Let's do it again after we eat."

186

"Sure," said the girl.

Weber went over and picked up the two pistols. They were still where he had left them. He thrust them both into his belt. "Bang, bang!" he said to Boo Brown. "Hey, weren't you tempted, with these things just laying there in easy reach?"

"Not me," said the musician. "I leave that stuff to Matt Dillon."

"Well, I'm going to wash up," Weber said. "Don't worry, Angie, I'll be back in a flash." He went to the usable forward rest room and locked himself inside.

"Why didn't you take those guns?" Jenny demanded. "What do you think I got him to put them over there for?"

Boo shook his head. "Nope," he said. "He was testing me. I don't know what he had in mind. But you notice he's still got that grenade in his hip pocket."

"Why would he want to force a showdown?" Angie asked.

"I don't know. But I don't aim to play his game. Listen, you girls are handling it just right. Keep treating him like the boss, and he'll stay cool. But don't go grabbing for any of those guns. I think he wants us to force him into doing something to keep this plane from landing at Moscow. He's as scared of those Ruskies as he was of the fuzz in Seattle."

Jerry Weber returned. "Hey," he said sitting down, "this looks great."

"Got any wine?" Boo asked.

"Burgundy or white?"

"Burgundy," said the musician. "Let's have us a party."

"I'll get it right away," said the stewardess.

187

"Angie," Weber called after her.

"Yes?"

"Go ahead and give that FBI man something to eat. I don't mind."

"I will," she said.

"I know he seems rational now," Paul Manchester said, leaning across the high frequency radio to speak directly to O'Hara, "but look at what's happened. He diverted you from San Francisco to Seattle. Then he wanted to go to Okinawa. Now it's Moscow. He could keep this up until the wings fall off. What do you do in Moscow if he decides he'd like to see India? I say we've got to surprise him and get him under control."

"It's my decision to make," O'Hara said. "And right now, I don't feel like making it. That's why I came up here to talk with you. That act you pulled back in Fairbanks could have blown the whistle on all of us. Now I know you're worried about Angie, but I've got everyone on this plane to think about. So lay off. Or you'll find yourself sitting back there with J. Edgar Hoover."

"I think you're wrong," Manchester said, glad that he had not mentioned the pistol to anyone.

"I can't eat another bite," Jerry Weber said, pushing his plate away. "Angie, you're the best cook I ever met."

"How about some ice cream?"

He laughed and nodded his head toward the white expanse below the windows. "Save it for the polar bears," he said. Then he yawned. "Man," he said, "you know what I'd like to do?"

"What?" Boo Brown asked.

"Take a nap," Weber answered.

"Why don't you?" said Angela Shaw.

In Leningrad a Russian officer pushed a button and brought the nine air bases and the eighteen surface to air missile sites along the Baltic to Red Alert.

## THE SEVENTEENTH HOUR

"I think I'll go back and get some coffee," Paul Manchester said, yawning. "Anybody else want some?"

No one did. He stood, stretched, and opened the door into the passenger compartment.

What he saw froze him for a moment, then he closed the door slowly behind him and moved carefully along the corridor between the rest rooms and the lounge area.

Stretched out in a seat that had been tilted all the way back, lips slack, rippling the air with a gentle snore, Jerry Weber slept.

Manchester pulled out his shirt tail and extracted the flat pistol from the small of his back. He examined the safety carefully to be sure it was off, then put the gun down along his leg and started toward the sleeping man.

A hand caught his wrist. He whirled. It was Angela.

"No, Paul!" she whispered.

"I'm not going to hurt him," he hissed back. "But once

I get him disarmed we can turn back for the States."

"Do you know what could happen if a bullet went through the hull at this altitude? The plane might explode like a balloon."

"We have to take that chance. Do you know that the Russians are threatening to shoot us down?" He moved toward the sleeping man.

Grimly she said, "I won't let you."

He stared at her. "For Christ's sake, why not? Are you on his side?"

"I'm not on anyone's side. But I promised no one would hurt him."

"You don't make promises to a criminal. Angie, let go of my arm. He might wake up any minute."

A ragged tear to her voice, Angela Shaw told him, "Paul, if you take another step I'm going to scream and he *will* wake up."

"I don't believe what I'm hearing," Manchester said. "Do you want me to get shot?"

"Paul, please," she said. "I don't want anyone to get shot. Now will you go up forward again and leave him alone? What you're doing is too dangerous for all of us."

"No," he said.

She stepped away from him and as her lips parted he knew suddenly that she had not been bluffing, that she was going to scream and he wanted to call back the words that had just passed between them but it was too late. He started to lift the pistol . . .

The doctor came out of the Intensive Cardiac Care Unit at Manhattan's St. Vincent's Hospital and shook hands with Herbert Kean.

"We think it was just a spasm," said the doctor. "The

cardiograph is normal, and his pulse and color are good. But just to be safe we're administering anticoagulants and we'll keep General Hotchkiss on the machines overnight. Are you his son?"

"In a way," said Kean. He thanked the doctor and settled down for the long wait.

Then Boo Brown was standing in the aisle, his big black fingers wrapped around Paul Manchester's hand and the flat pistol.

"Man, you don't want to rock the boat after all we've been through," the musician said softly, plucking the pistol from Manchester's fingers like an apple from a branch.

Behind him, Weber sprang up, eyes blinking sleepily. "Hey, what's all the fuss?" he demanded.

As he slipped the pistol deftly into his hip pocket, Boo turned and said, "No fuss, buddy. This cat just came back for some more chow. He must have a tapeworm."

Weber pushed between them. His eyes were cold and seemed to bore into Manchester's brain. "You're supposed to be working," the young soldier said. "The whole idea was to give the regular crew a rest. Now why don't you get back up there where you belong and let these people take it easy? They've been in the air since seven this morning."

Manchester looked at Angie. "I'm sorry," he said.

She turned away without answering. He pushed past Boo Brown and went back to the flight deck.

Weber yawned. "I ought to know better than to take a nap," he said.

"Why?" Boo asked, wondering how much the boy had heard.

"Because I always feel worse when I get up," Weber said. "Come on, let's get some coffee. I'll make it. Give poor Angie a rest."

The big black musician and the young soldier crowded into the forward galley and as the Boeing 707 passed over the North Pole, Boo Brown spooned out fresh coffee while the hijacker heated the water.

## THE EIGHTEENTH HOUR   E S T

As Flight 901 sped above the Arctic Ocean, the hours seemed to tumble over themselves. In the rear compartment the young FBI agent slept. Near him, tired of reading, John Bimonte tried to forget his exile by playing solitaire with a deck of Trans-America cards.

Farther up the aisle, where he had removed the arm rests from a row of three seats, First Officer Sam Allen dozed. His left foot twitched as he dreamed of some long-ago day when he had kicked the winning field goal for Penn State against Ohio.

Captain Michael O'Hara did not sleep; he roved from the flight deck to the rear galley, eyes questing, ears probing. O'Hara was not a man who relaxed when things became quiet.

Angela Shaw sat in a First Class seat, eyes half-closed. She had shut the partition between the First Class and Tourist cabins. At Jerry Weber's request she put on a jazz tape cassette, and as its flourishing trumpets and rapid piano seeped through the airplane, Boo Brown began to unpack his cello.

Weber sat with Jenny O'Hara. They both watched the musician intensely.

It was obvious that this was a ritual with him. He placed the case across his knees and stroked it as if it were a living creature. Then slowly—carefully—he inserted a key into the lock and turned until there was a quiet click. He removed the key and placed it back in a special pouch in his wallet and returned the wallet to his breast coat pocket. Now it was time to unsnap the latches. He did them one at a time, pausing between each, and at last the lid was free to open.

He lifted it just a few inches and peered inside. "How are you doing, Mama?" he asked. Prolonging the ritual, he lifted the lid further and tilted his huge face until he had placed his nose and one cheek inside. "Mmmm," he said, "you do smell good!" Now he opened the lid fully and reached inside with both hands.

The cello was a deep, rich brown, venerable with age and mellow with wax. As he lifted it out, Jenny went, "Ohhh!" Boo beamed a smile at her. He placed the cello on the seat next to him and removed a bow from the case. He tested its surface with his thumb, then applied a coating of resin. "Mama likes 'em rough," he said. He cocked one ear at the music coming from the hi fi system. "This stuff's kind of funky," he said, "but I guess me and Mama can sing along with it."

The music paused, and a new piece began. "Hey, now," Boo said, "that's more like it. That's Dave Brubeck's 'Audrey.' You know how that one started? Some photographer cat, Gjon Mili, was studying the Brubeck Quartet for a movie he wanted to make, and Gjon raised his hands at a recording session and said, 'Fellows, I would like to see Audrey Hepburn come walking through the woods.' Paul Desmond, who was blowing sax said, 'Gee, so would I,' and old Dave, he said, 'One, two three' . . ."

As Boo finished, the music surged, Brubeck's Mozartian piano backed softly by a double bass, and then Desmond's sax. The number was so complete within itself that it scemed impossible that Boo Brown could do anything with his cello but destroy the mood. But when he began to play, with his fingers at first, and then with the bow, it was as if he and Paul Desmond and Dave Brubeck were sitting together in the First Class lounge of Flight 901, jamming together at midnight . . .

## THE NINETEENTH HOUR     E S T

"Here they come," said O'Hara, studying the radar scope. Sam Allen leaned over his shoulder and studied the white blips against the green field.

"That's the wrong direction," he said. "That's not theirs, it's ours!"

O'Hara tapped the co-pilot on the shoulder, and when the man got up slipped into the right seat. He put on the earphones, picked up the microphone.

"This is Trans-America 901," he said. "Unidentified traffic, please check in. Over."

"901, this is Alpha Bravo Niner," said a drawling voice. "We thought you might like some company."

"Are you Air Force? Over."

"Well, we aren't Coast Guard," said the voice.

"Alpha Bravo Niner," said O'Hara, "I don't understand. Are you escorting us, or what? Over."

"Let's say," the voice replied, "that we're walking you

through the park, so any muggers in the area will think twice."

"Negative," said O'Hara. "Listen, thanks, but if we're going to get through at all it's because we're what we seem to be, unarmed and civilian. Shear off!"

"Just trying to be friendly," said the voice.

"Many thanks," O'Hara replied. "I mean it. But we're better off by ourselves."

"Okay," said the voice, "it's your airplane, mister. I just hope you're right."

O'Hara looked out the window and saw three distant contrails, doubling back on themselves.

"So do I," he said.

"Hey," said Boo Brown, listening to a new selection from the tape player, "We really lucked into it tonight. That's Eddie Condon's 'Home Cooking.' We call that Chicago jazz."

"What's Brubeck?" asked Jenny O'Hara.

Boo Brown laughed. "You won't believe it, honey," he said, "but when Dave was really making it, back in the fifties, they called him 'Modern.' "

He strummed the strings of the cello. "Come on, mama," he murmured, "let's show these folks what soul is."

As he played, Jenny and Weber talked quietly.

"What are you going to do now?" she asked.

"I wish I knew," he said. "They ought to be able to use me for something. I mean, there's always room for a good heavy weapons man."

"You wouldn't give away secrets!"

"There's nothing secret about the stuff I used," he said. "But it takes skill to make it work. I guess I could train

198

guys, or something."

"Jerry," she said, "why don't you come back to the United States with us? I know it makes everything that's happened seem kind of silly, but it really would be better for you. You'd have to be punished, we both know that, but all of us would testify in your behalf."

"Jenny, I can't," he said, a painful expression twisting his face. "They'd shoot me. Or else lock me up for keeps."

"Not after all you did for that woman and her baby," she said. "And you could have left that FBI man down there in the bottom of the plane to freeze. But you didn't. Oh, Jerry, I wish you'd listen to me."

"Do you?" he said softly. "Are you asking me to listen?"

"Yes, oh yes!" she whispered.

He forced a smile. "Well," he said, "I'm always complaining that people don't listen to *me*. So I guess I'd better practice what I preach, don't you think?"

She clutched his arm. "Does that mean you'll do it?"

"Maybe," he said slowly. "I have to think about it. And I want to talk to the Captain. But maybe."

She leaned forward and brushed a furtive kiss against his cheek. Engrossed in his music, Boo Brown still did not miss it.


"These aren't ours," said Sam Allen, leaning over the radar scope. "And they're closing fast."

"Throttle back," O'Hara told the new pilot.

"What are you doing?" Allen asked.

"I see them," said the new pilot. "Three—no, four. Dead ahead."

"Air speed 225," said O'Hara. "220. 215."

"What the hell—" began Sam Allen.

"Gear down," called O'Hara.

"Gear down," repeated the new pilot. The jet shuddered as the wheel wells opened and the heavy landing gear ripped into the resisting air. The plane yawed and slowed.

"Soviet Air Commander," O'Hara called, on the international distress frequency, "we are an unarmed, civilian airliner, forced off course by a hijacker. I have lowered my wheels. Do you read me? This is Trans-America Flight 901. Over to you."

"I read you," said an accented voice. "Please be advised, we have just received orders to escort you to Moscow Airport. You may retract your landing gear. Over."

"Thank you," said O'Hara. He cradled the microphone, gave a tearing, heaving sigh and, looking out at the distance of the sky, repeated softly, "Thank you."

Paul Manchester slid into the seat beside Angela Shaw. "Hi," he said.

"Oh, Paul," she said. "Why did you have to come to Fairbanks?"

"I was trying to help," he said.

"But you nearly ruined everything. How could you be so stupid? Sneaking on board with a gun and pretending to be a pilot. You could have gotten us all killed."

"I love you," he said. "I didn't think of anything but trying to protect you. If I was wrong, I'm sorry. But I think I'd do it again."

"Yes, you would," she said. "Paul, we're on different wave lengths. You're an, oh I don't know, adventuresome, colorful guy. Me, I'm just plain Jane, getting my kicks by pretending flying is exciting and sort of dangerous, when it's nothing of the kind. My racket is broiling steaks and mixing drinks. You want someone with long red hair who rides horses and wouldn't think of having a baby before she was thirty." She looked down at her cigarette. "Isn't that funny. Here all along I thought I was the one who wanted the excitement. But it turns out the other way around."

He was silent. She touched his cheek.

"Be honest," she said quietly, "aren't you glad we found out now instead of later?"

It was 9:00 A.M. in Moscow, and the city was gray and silent under its blanket of snow. Few cars moved along the streets, and those that did were like black hearses gliding noiselessly along the icy thoroughfares.

Moscow Control had picked up Flight 901 in its long-range radar room. Two Sukhoi delta-winged fighters had been dispatched to join the interceptors already shepherding the Boeing 707 into the letdown area.

At Moscow Airport, contingents of security police formed up. A temporary debarking area well away from the main terminal was set up with a portable ramp and a large trailer containing two main rooms, a toilet, and a kitchenette.

The security police joked among themselves. One frequently repeated phrase was "Havana, U.S.S.R."

"What do you think will happen to me?" Weber asked.

Honestly, Captain Michael O'Hara said, "I don't know. In view of the circumstances, I think you'll get off fairly light. But that could still mean a few years in prison. I don't want to kid you, son."

"That's why I asked you," Weber said. "Isn't it too bad you and me couldn't have talked back in New York? I bet you would have figured out something for me to do before I got myself in all this trouble."

"That's in the past," O'Hara said. "Okay, Jerry, if I can help you I will. But I'll have to turn you over to the authorities, you know that."

"All right," Weber said. "But ours, not the Russians."

"I'll do the best I can," O'Hara told him. "I've already radioed ahead to have the American Ambassador waiting for us. I'll do everything possible to have you placed in his custody."

"You've got to," Weber said. "Listen, I don't know. Maybe I'm sick. I look back on what I did today and I don't understand why. At the time it seemed right, but now I know it wasn't. I don't know what the hell I'd do if the Russians wanted me to teach them about our weapons. I don't trust myself anymore."

O'Hara spread his hands. "If you want to trust me," he said, "I won't let you down. I'll go all the way for you."

"That's good enough for me," said Jerry Weber. He fumbled in his pockets and began handing his weapons over to the Captain.

O'Hara took the two pistols and then the grenade. He held them awkwardly.

"I'll keep these for you," he said finally.

"No rush," said Weber. He tried to smile. "I won't be needing them for at least five years."

A.M.

## THE TWENTIETH HOUR          E S T

They had passed over Vyshniy Volochek and Kalinin, and were on course for Moscow Airport. The two Sukhoi fighters had been on their wing since they crossed the finger of the White Sea that terminates at Kandalaksha. They were sleek, professional-looking aircraft, all airfoil and missile brackets, manned by oxygen-masked pilots who stared impassively at the 707.

O'Hara and Allen had relieved the temporary pilots and were going through their landing check list.

"Do you have any idea," the First Officer asked, "what this is going to do to our flight hours this month? I'm already nine hours over my maximum allowance. The overtime's nice, but the dispatcher's going to scream bloody murder. They may make us walk home."

O'Hara did not answer. "Flaps thirty degrees," he said.

"Flaps thirty," Allen replied.

203

The jet shuddered slightly as the wing surface increased.

"220 indicated," said Allen.

"Gear down," said O'Hara.

Sam Allen moved the lever, the giant doors beneath the plane snapped open, and a mass of air washed against the plane like a monstrous waterfall.

"Nose gear locked," Allen said. "All green."

On his final approach, at a thousand feet, O'Hara saw that the air speed was 170 miles an hour. The long, broad runway was directly ahead. At its near end, a highway ran alongside a fence. It was almost empty: only three cars were in sight.

"Full flaps," O'Hara commanded.

Allen pulled the flap handle all the way back. "Full flaps," he reported.

The jet slowed; as it crossed the highway and searched for the runway with its groping wheels, the air speed indicator read 156 miles an hour. The main gear hit first, and O'Hara immediately shoved the yoke forward to bring down the nose wheels. As they squealed against the concrete, he pulled back on the speed brake handle and, along the tops of both wings, spoilers rose sixty degrees, destroying the air flow and setting up a braking surface. The throttles were in "idle" now, and above them, in O'Hara's strong fingers, were the reverse thrust levers. He pulled them back and huge doors slammed shut at the rear of the four jet engines, forcing the fiery blast forward like a retro-rocket to slow the plane.

At sixty miles an hour, he turned the 707 off the runway onto a taxi strip where a blue truck waited, flying a checkered flag. Its driver leaned out and waved. The signal was unmistakable. "Follow me."

"Flaps up," O'Hara said. He dropped the spoilers back into place and, on minimum power, followed the truck.

In the rear cabin John Bimonte untied William Reading's hands. The young FBI man rubbed his wrists. "Thanks," he said.

Bimonte said nothing. He was wondering what he was going to say to Michael O'Hara.

Boo Brown tucked the cello gently into its case. "I'm sorry I didn't get a chance to play more," he told Jerry Weber. "But I'll send you some of my records."

"Sure," said Jerry. "You do that."

Jenny O'Hara reached over and held his hand. "I'm glad you decided to listen to me," she said. "It'll be better this way, you just wait and see."

Paul Manchester sat awkwardly beside Angela Shaw. "I want another chance," he said. "This isn't exactly what I had in mind."

She touched his cheek. "Poor Paul," she said. "You saw yourself on a white charger, riding to the aid of the damsel in distress, and when you got there, all she could say was 'Buzz off, I'm not interested.' I'm sorry."

"But you don't just end something like this, Angie," he said.

"Oh, Paul," she said, "don't you see? It never began."

"We'll see," he said calmly.

The two relief pilots sat quietly in the last row of First Class seats. One said to the other, "This hijacking crap has got to come to a screeching halt."

"Amen," said the other.

The plane followed the truck to the trailer parked half a mile from the terminal building.

Allen shut down the emergency exit lights, switched off

the cockpit window heaters, closed down the deicing equipment, cut power to the galleys, and threw all but one of the main circuit breakers.

O'Hara locked the parking brakes and shut down three of the engines. The fourth was kept running to provide electrical power until a ground cart could be plugged in. He looked down from his window, fifteen feet above the ground, and saw the Russian crew pushing a portable ramp toward the forward hatch.

"Well," he said, "we have arrived."

At St. Vincent's Hospital in New York, an orderly tapped the dozing Herbert Kean on his shoulder.

"Mr. Kean? You can go home now."

"What?" Kean mumbled. "How is the General?"

"We've put him to sleep," said the orderly. "But there's no danger. The last thing he said was to tell you to see that Mike O'Hara gets a week off. Does that mean anything to you?"

"Yeah," Herbert Kean said, tightening his necktie. "It means the General is back in the saddle again."

The main hatch, sealed pluglike in its socket, moved inward and then to one side. A uniformed man stepped inside, accompanied by a blast of chill air.

"Are you the Captain?" he asked Sam Allen, who was just emerging from the flight deck. Sam jerked his head over one shoulder toward O'Hara, who was just behind him.

"Yes?" said O'Hara.

"The Union of Soviet Socialist Republics welcomes you," said the man, saluting. "We are sorry that you were forced to make this visit under such unpleasant circumstances. Would you please instruct your passengers to de-plane, sir?"

"Sure," said O'Hara. "We're a little tired of this crate anyway." He picked up the announcement microphone and said, "Okay, folks, this is the end of the line. If you'll file down the ramp I see they've got a trailer waiting for us and, with any luck at all, some better coffee than the stuff *we* serve."

"Will you point the hijacker out to me?" the official said softly, almost into his ear.

O'Hara looked at him blandly. "What hijacker?" he asked.

The American Ambassador had been delayed by a flat tire. As his car sped out the taxiway, he could see the Trans-America jet parked near a gray trailer. A group of people stood under its wing.

The Soviet official had refused to allow the passengers and crew to enter the trailer until he knew which one was "the criminal."

"Hijacking is a capital offense," he said. "Only the fact that this aircraft was in distress caused us to permit it to overfly our borders. Now you say there is no hijacker? I find this difficult to accept."

William Reading, who had been about to say something, found his foot trodden on heavily by Boo Brown. "Let's keep it in the family," said the musician.

"You will submit to search," decided the official. There were protests, but the squad of security policeman moved in, automatic rifles at the ready. The official reached for Boo's cello case. The musician yanked it back. "What is inside that?" asked the official.

"I'll open it," said Boo. He did, and as he started to remove the cello, one of the security policemen snatched the instrument from his hands. Boo grabbed its neck. "Hey, there!" he yelled. "That's mine!"

The official said something in Russian. The policeman released the cello and stepped back.

"Give," the official said, reaching for Jerry Weber's cloth suitcase.

The young soldier pulled away.

"Better let him have it," Boo said.

"You said you wouldn't let them hurt me!" Weber said hoarsely.

Alarmed, Boo Brown stepped toward the boy. "Simmer down, buddy," he said. "These cats don't know the score."

But Weber did not seem to hear him. He threw open the suitcase, which was unzipped, and reached inside.

The small submachine gun—a "grease gun," little more than a snub barrel, a chamber, and a folding stock —came out of the suitcase. Weber's hand snapped the cocking lever back and his finger sought the cast metal trigger.

"Oh, my God, *no!*" yelled Boo Brown. "Drop it, Jerry! They'll kill you!" As the grease gun was coming to bear on the Russian official the black musician took one step forward and, seeing that he was still too far away to grab the weapon, took a violent swing with his cello and smashed it—fragile sounding board, brown-varnished neck, taut strings that snapped in all directions—against Jerry Weber's arm and the machine gun. The weapon clattered to the concrete, surrounded by bits of shattered wood.

"You lied to me!" Weber said softly. He turned and ran under the jet. The security policemen rushed forward and O'Hara leaped in front of them, waving his hands. "He's unarmed!" the pilot shouted.

But the Russians did not hear, or did not understand, or did not care. The guns were already firing.

Jerry Weber stopped running near one of the huge landing gear dollies. Several bullets hit the tires, and they blew out with a noise louder than the shots. The plane lurched and one wing settled toward the runway. Weber put one hand against the tattered rubber and, as if he were seeking a soft place to sleep, lowered himself slowly to the oil-stained concrete.

## EPILOGUE

Hours later, Boo Brown walked out to the jet plane and stood near its ramp, kicking at what was left of his cello.

Angela Shaw came out and stood near him.

"Boo," she said, "I'm sorry. You lost your wonderful instrument."

He looked at her and his eyes were glistening with tears.

"Angie," he said, "I lost a whole lot more than that. I gave him my word. My solemn word."